RUSTLERS' MOON

Private investigator Bart Hall was in prison in Colorado, on an under-cover job, when he first encountered outlaw Jake Harris, who had a curious symbol tattooed on the back of his hand: a letter 'H' in a circle. When a ring bearing the same symbol reached him from his deceased stepfather, Bart sought the Circle H ranch in Texas, where he quickly became involved in a family feud. Small scale rustling got out of hand, and Bart flirted with death on several occasions before the big showdown.

Books by David Bingley
in the Linford Western Library:

BRIGAND'S BOUNTY
TROUBLESHOOTERS ON TRIAL
GREENHORN GORGE

DAVID BINGLEY

RUSTLERS' MOON

Complete and Unabridged

LINFORD
Leicester

First published in Great Britain in 1972

First Linford Edition
published 2003

British Library CIP Data

Bingley, David, *1920 –*
    Rustlers' moon.—Large print ed.—
Linford western library
1. Western stories
2. Large type books
I. Title
823.9'14 [F]

ISBN 1–8439–5025–1

Published by
F. A. Thorpe (Publishing)
Anstey, Leicestershire

Set by Words & Graphics Ltd.
Anstey, Leicestershire
Printed and bound in Great Britain by
T. J. International Ltd., Padstow, Cornwall

1

La Junta County Prison in the state of Colorado, was a grim, solid building fashioned out of local limestone. Its walls were two feet thick with narrow slits of window opening on to the cells. Not much fresh air got into the prisoners' quarters and very little daylight penetrated to them.

Bart Hall, a young investigator from Dodge City, in the neighbouring state of Kansas, had been one of the inmates for three days. In far less than seventy-two hours he had felt and realised all the drawbacks, and he fervently hoped — on the third afternoon of his stay — that his mission, that of winning certain information from a long-term prisoner, would soon be accomplished.

Bart had been given a criminal record to pass him off as a renegade.

The jailor had let it be known that he was wanted for serious crimes in a county further west, and that he had been moved to this prison to prevent his fellow outlaws from finding him and breaking him out of jail.

Every man had a cell to himself. When they were indoors, it had been comparatively easy for Bart to emulate an ordinary prisoner, but out in the open the subterfuge was a little more difficult.

On that third hot day, he was down the quarrying slope along with a dozen other men in drab prison denims, cutting out and breaking down large quantities of heavy granite. The convicts were spread about in small groups. One other man, a person named Jake Harris, shared the particular pile of rock upon which Bart was working.

A huge slab of granite, ten feet in height, towered between them, so that neither could see the other without moving sideways. Bart was glad of this, because Harris had a peculiarly penetrating gaze and he had shown no signs of friendliness since Bart was assigned to work near him.

Every now and then, Bart paused between swings of his pick. His hands were by no means excessively soft and yet the constant working with heavy tools on materials as hard as granite had taken a toll of him. He was afraid that some knowing prisoner would decide that he did not have the tough skin of a long-term inmate.

Bart turned and glanced up the slope behind him. In a prominent position, Warder Trass, a tall figure with a greying moustache, in a dark baggy uniform, contemplated the workers. His big hands shifted a heavy wooden truncheon from the left to the right. The whistle on the long silver chain swung a little as he moved. His long-barrelled revolver was worn in a holster towards the front of his coat.

Bart sighed and licked in a trickle of perspiration. At twenty-eight he was quite mature; a tall, handsome young fellow with a long face and pale blue eyes which missed very little. His customary alertness was not always obvious because his eyes were deep set under straight black brows.

His muscular frame could have been that of a cattle man. During the three years since he moved from the eastern seaboard of the United States to Kansas, he had acquired many of the skills which westerners and men of the frontiers admired. These facilities had served him well in his rather risky profession of investigator.

He yawned, stroked his damp forehead with his forearm and prepared to swing his pick again. At the same time, he reflected how unsuitable the prison clothes were for this sort of physical exercise.

'Ho, there! Trass!'

A bellowing voice which carried with ease startled the watching warder out of his state of calmness. Trass turned about and raised his truncheon in salute to someone invisible to the prisoners on account of the hilltop.

'Yes, sir, Mr Gullett, sir? What can I do for you?'

Trass raised his voice but it in no way matched that of his superior, Jailor Moss Gullett. As his back turned, so the perspiring men relaxed in their labours and wondered what was afoot. Gullett never shouted like that unless there was a summons in the offing.

'I want Roxy Brownwood up here as soon as you can fix it. He has a visitor. Make it quick, *pronto*, you understand?'

'I get the message, Mr Gullett! He won't keep you waitin' long,' Trass promised.

The prisoner in question, Roxy Brownwood, let out a sudden roar of rage. Of the score or so of men housed in the prison, Brownwood was the one man foolish enough or reckless enough to display a show of temper when he felt like it. Warder Trass moved closer to the convict with his stick raised. This act was for the benefit of the jailor, in the event that he was still looking on.

Trass knew that a blow or two of the stick would in no way make Brownwood change his mind, if he decided to be obstinate. Only the nearest of the working party could hear the warder talking with a plea in his voice.

Brownwood made more noise. 'Ain't nothin' in the prison regulations says a man doin' time here has to give up his work to go an' talk to visitin' strangers, warder. I hope I knows my rights!'

The warder was feeling very uncertain of himself. A belated suggestion changed the whole situation.

'If you like you can take off his leg shackle! Seein' as how we're in a hurry, Trass.'

This time, Trass did not raise his voice to call back to the jailor. Instead, he renewed his pleading and advanced closer to Roxy with his key held out in front of him like a dagger used defensively. Suddenly, the notorious bank heister threw back his head and roared with laughter. He tossed down his digging tool, narrowly missing the legs of poor Trass. Brownwood clapped his hands to his chest and laughed some more. His ruddy face, camouflaged with the greying black beard, was clearly visible to most of the onlookers.

Brownwood allowed his keeper to free his leg. He then pretended to aim a kick at him and followed up by swinging the loose length of chain between his wrists in such a way that the warder had to skip back.

Roxy was so happy to be free of his leg shackle that he started off up the hill, half-running.

'Mind that chain doesn't get you into more trouble, Brownwood, an' mind you're polite to the visitor, whoever he is!'

Now that the unpredictable one was at a good distance, the warder had recovered his composure. He turned sharply and caught sight of his other charges leaning upon their tools.

'Now then, you men, what do you think this is, a fête day or something?

Bend your backs an' get workin' unless you want to feel the weight of my stick!'

Trass kicked a few stones away from his boots and walked solidly towards one group, as though to implement his threat, but no one came to any harm. If the truth were known, Warder Trass was as curious to know who had come to see Brownwood as was any one of his charges.

Roxy was the man Bart had hoped to have a private talk with, and thus far his efforts had not amounted to anything. Jailor Gullett knew young Hall's secret identity, but it was kept from Warder Trass. Consequently, Bart was having to make his own openings. As he applied himself to his work once again, he decided to try and learn something from his workmate.

'Is Roxy any sort of special friend of yours, Jake?'

There was a pause. Harris made a couple of swings before he elected to answer from the other side of the stack. 'Nope, I can't say he is. If the truth's known, Brownwood don't have any real friends in here at all. Nobody can stand him. You ever worked with him?'

'Nope, never. Can't say I feel I've missed much. It kind of makes a man curious, though, when such a galoot is permitted special visitors.'

'It may not be anyone Roxy wants to talk to. One way an' another, the authorities have been tryin' to get information out of him for many a year.'

Bart frowned at the rock face. He knew the truth of the statement he had just heard. 'What is it that he knows that they want to know?'

'A bank heister, an' you have to ask a question like that?'

Jake Harris spat against the face of the rock on his side, and at that moment in time the conversation faded.

★   ★   ★

Roxy Brownwood came down the slope just over an hour later, followed at a safe economic distance by Jailor Gullett. The prisoner was grinning rather indifferently. He had obviously got some sort of pleasure out of the visit. Gullett, on the other hand, had his jaws so clenched that the muscles stood out, even on a face as round as his. The jailor was a stocky, barrel-chested man who had once served his country at sea. His deep-sea roll was exaggerated on this occasion.

'Mr Trass, give Brownwood five minutes to recover his poise and then put the shackle back on him. Maybe a shift of position might do him good.'

Gullett winked at his subordinate and indicated by the direction of a glance where he wanted Brownwood to go. Trass seemed momentarily surprised, but he reacted quickly, and before some of the workers had the time to look around unnoticed, Roxy was on his way to join Harris and young Hall. The latter was so surprised that he was afraid his expression might give him away.

Gullett gave a long, hard look at Hall, but the young investigator refused to look back at him in case Harris noticed anything untoward. Closely watched by the warder and the jailor, Brownwood picked up a long-handled pick and swung it about him as though checking upon the weight of it. He seemed pleased, and without waiting for further instruction, he moved to Bart's side of the heap and commenced work there. The shape of the hollow made it difficult for two tall men to work on the obvious spot at that side. Bart tried swinging so that his pick went in when Roxy was pulling back, but the bearded man was so erratic that Bart had to ease off, so as to prevent an accident.

No sooner was his pick still than Roxy wanted to talk to him.

'Know what all that was about, young fellow?'

'No, none of us know that. How about tellin' me before Trass gets back?'

Gullett had retreated up the hill, and Trass had gone part of the way with him, still talking.

'That there was a federal officer waitin' to speak to me. Know what he wanted?' Bart shook his head, although he could have guessed without difficulty. 'He wanted to know where my brother is, 'cause my brother Pete is supposed to know where the missin' loot is from a raid in Santa Fé. Pete ain't rightly the man to ask 'cause he's been dead this two years, killed in a knifin' incident with a Mex whose wife he made off with.

'But that there officer, U.S. Marshal French, is goin' to make a special journey, all the way to Las Vegas, jest to get in touch with my brother, an' to do that, he'll have to dig him up. Don't you think that's kind of funny, young fellow? I do, especially as I might get a little time off my sentence for comin' through with the information.'

'Brownwood, that'll be 'nough talk from you,' Trass remarked heavily. The chain and ball was dumped at Roxy's feet. 'Get that hoop of metal round your ankle an' don't take all day in doin' it. Some way or another, Jailor Gullett don't seem to be as pleased with you as you do yourself. You hear me, fix it!'

Brownwood rubbed the perspiration off his beard. He stared at Trass as though he could not believe his ears, but the warder did not wilt under his stare. Instead, he hooked a toe under the ball and made it roll sharply against the prisoner's ankle. Trass bent down, very watchful for any sort of trickery, and the band of iron was soon in place.

'Now you're ready to start, I'd take it as a favour if you'd apply yourself to this side of the rock.'

Trass again moved the ball sharply with his foot. This caused the shackle to dig into Brownwood's ankle, a spot which is always painful to men thus hobbled. Brownwood cursed, and half bent down, but he limped around the other side of the rock, and presently, over his own exertions, Bart became aware that both picks on the other side were swinging.

The quarrel started about ten minutes later. During that initial period neither Brownwood nor Harris had exchanged a word. Roxy uttered a sharp protest. One pick continued to swing, and then came the retort followed by the sounds of blows and the ominous rattle of chains being pulled quickly this way and that.

Bart did not want to bring Trass into what was happening. If he acted without instructions, however, he might be dished out with some fearful fatigue before he managed to regain his freedom. Tossing down his tool, he hurried around the rock mass, hauling on his ball and chain. He was in time to see Harris's head glance off the solid rock.

Harris looked groggy. Brownwood removed his hands from Harris's throat and bent to pick up a stone the size of his fist. As soon as he had straightened he started to hit his victim with the stone, and Harris had great difficulty in defending himself. One blow clipped the side of his temple. Another struck his right forearm with jarring force and a third slid down his left wrist.

Bart sprang forward. His chain was just long enough to let him get within grappling distance. He grabbed the arm of the bearded man as he aimed a fourth blow. The arm and fist were arrested, and Roxy was thrown off balance. Bart put a leg behind him, and he fell over it, rather heavily, losing the stone which he had used as a weapon.

Roxy started to roll aside and to contemplate an immediate attack upon his new adversary, but Bart was by then standing over him and menacing him with the metal ball attached to his own ankle. Brownwood spread his hands, having read the unspoken message in the younger man's eyes.

'Warder Trass, get yourself over here!'

This was the first time that most of the prisoners had heard Bart's voice raised. They were surprised at the apparent authority in it. Trass bounded along without hesitation. He came upon a situation which baffled him for a minute or more.

Bart cautiously stepped back. 'If you'll take charge of this ruffian, I'd like permission to take Harris down to the stream to bathe his wounds. He's hurt.'

Trass hesitated, wanting to check that things were as they seemed. Harris propped himself up, bareheaded, and gasping for breath. When he could talk he explained.

'He went a little wild because some stone dust went near his eyes. Swore I'd done it on purpose.'

Trass gave his permission and he stayed to admonish Brownwood while Bart and Jake Harris moved off to the bank of the shallow stream which was in full view from anyone above it. Bart really did help with the bruised skin around Harris's temple, but it was when the water cleansing session was almost over that the remarkable discovery was made.

On the back of Harris's bruised left hand was a design of sorts, put there by a tattoo artist. Bart knew it at once, in another connection. It was a capital 'H' in a circle. The sight of it at once took Bart's thoughts back to his earlier life on the east coast. His widowed mother had married again, and her second husband, a rancher from Texas, had had a ring on his finger. An ornate ring with exactly the same device upon it. A device said to represent the cattle brand of an outfit called the Circle H.

His expression clouded over as his thoughts went back to those days directly after his mother remarried. He had no great feeling for the western character who had become his step-father, and who had been the cause of his leaving home.

Bart's thoughts came back to the present, as Trass filled his lungs and ordered them back on the job.

2

When Bart turned in that night, he was more discontented than he had been since he first entered the awe-inspiring prison.

Jailor Gullett's visits to the cell blocks were few and far between, and although the visiting peace officer had apparently extracted from Brownwood what he thought to be the required information, the young investigator could not expect to be released immediately, in case the inmates guessed that he had been 'planted' in their midst. If Brownwood, for instance, found out Bart's true mission in life he was sufficiently unpredictable to start a riot of sorts.

At an early hour, Bart stretched out upon his hardboard bed and gently sniffed the unhealthy prison odour. Anyone who could endure an existence like this one for any length of time was a tough *hombre* indeed.

He wondered how many of the men in the prison would still be fit when they were released, and how many of them would still want to hit the trails and live the lives of men on the run. He thought that they would have to be conditioned to it, or be utterly desperate.

Presently, his eyes found it harder to focus. And yet he wanted to think. Somewhere beyond the prison, in the nearby town, was a federal officer named French who was prepared to make a journey to Las Vegas to try and find Roxy Brownwood's brother. If Bart could get out in time, he could save that officer a frustrating journey. Some would have said that putting in an undercover man at the same time as a federal officer appeared was overdoing it. Now, however, it could be shown that the federal man in Kansas, who had had Bart sent inside, had acted wisely.

Bart's thoughts ranged around this

ending to an old problem. He was not surprised when other considerations crowded the Brownwood business out of his mind. His half-closed eyes were seeing again that tattooed symbol on the back of Jake Harris's hand. The Circle H, it had been. There was no doubt about it. Bart's stepfather, the person who had had the same device upon his ring, had a similar name to the outlaw. His name was Harries. Brad Harries; Bradford Harries in reality.

Brad Harries had come from somewhere in northwest Texas. He had made that clear at the time when he courted Bart's mother. But did Jake Harris come from the same part of the world? Or had he merely copied the tattooing from something which had taken his fancy? After all, there might very well be more than one Circle H in the southern states of the Union.

In trying to match up Jake Harris with Brad Harries, ex-rancher, of Texas, Bart was involving his tired brain in mere idle speculation. He soon grew weary of the unrewarding exercise and fell asleep.

★   ★   ★

Release from prison came sooner than he had expected.

Around eight o'clock the following morning, Gullett had all the inmates lined up in the exercise yard and it was obvious that he had something on his mind. He cracked a riding whip, which he usually carried with him for show, and examined every man very closely although there had been no opportunities for sprucing up.

Trass was the one to give the order to pick up the metal balls. Each man did as he was told, and soon the dead weight of the balls began to have an effect. The men began to perspire, and that was before the gruelling day's work had begun.

Presently, Gullett positioned himself in front of the double line of glowering men and started to unburden himself.

'There's a man standing in front of me who is no doubt feelin' pleased with himself, a man whose renegade friends on the outside are reputed to be interested in breakin' him out. Well, I have news for him. No one has ever broken out of this prison in my time.

'Nor is it goin' to start now.'

Gullett took a few steps to one side, his eyes ranging along the lines of inmates, and then he walked back the other way. Excitement was rife among the ranks. Upwards of half a dozen men had it in mind that they were likely to be freed. Roxy clearly had the idea; so had Jake Harris, if the brightness of his eyes was anything to go by.

'I shall ensure that no one will interfere with the smooth runnin' of this model jail by havin' the man transferred to another institution. He's already been moved once, but seemingly that is not enough. I'm referrin' to a man who was involved in an incident yesterday afternoon.

'No, not you, Brownwood, an' not

Harris, either. I mean the other man, standin' in between you. The name we had given for him was Calvin Arthur, though I doubt very much if that was the one given to him by his mother. Are you hearin' well, Arthur?'

Bart coloured up a little and hung his head before nodding it. He had drawn unnecessary attention to himself by forgetting the name he had assumed. Now, he started to put on an act, shifting his feet and smirking as though he was pleased with his own notoriety.

'Mr Trass, you'll dismiss the parade right away, but I want our friend Arthur in my office in five minutes.'

There were quiet jeers and a lot of side-glances and leering as the yard was cleared. Bart, however, ignored most of it and he began to feel better as soon as he was in the jailor's private office. There, Gullett shook him by the hand and offered him a small cigar.

'The tumbleweed wagon is outside the house at the front. I'll put you in it and start you back on the road to freedom in a minute or two, but I wanted to ask if you'd found out anything from Brownwood after we had him up here yesterday. Take a seat.'

Bart nodded and explained all that Roxy had said to him after he came back from the office. Gullett was a shrewd character. He was in no way surprised when Bart made it clear that the prisoner had hoodwinked the visiting officer.

'I tried to tell him how tricky Roxy could be, but he wouldn't believe me. Now, he'll have to be disappointed, and that quite soon. He's supposed to be setting off for Vegas around ten o'clock.'

Bart coughed on the tobacco smoke. He was restless now. 'I'll tell him all there is to know as soon as I make contact. I suppose the lock-up wagon will take me some distance out of town before I assume my own identity?'

Gullett came to his feet, confirming Bart's ideas. They parted amicably. The wagon carried the prisoner half a mile beyond the town, where a local deputy was waiting with Bart's horse and regular gear. The young investigator moved into trailside bushes and made the transformation while the wagon turned around and went back to the prison.

'Jailor Gullett runs a tough prison, so they tell me,' the deputy opined.

'I can confirm that, if confirmation is wanted,' Bart assured him.

Five minutes later, he stepped out on to the trail again in his usual everyday working and riding outfit. The prison garb he kicked before him into the dust of the trail. He had on a blue shirt, done up at the neck under a black string tie. His hat was a flat-crowned black one with a snakeskin band. A lightweight grey jacket partially hid the .45 Colt worn over his right hip. Good-quality denims and black hide boots completed his rigout and the transformation.

'Clothes sure do change a man,' the deputy remarked, with admiration in his voice.

The high-stepping dun quarter horse which had been brought along for Bart began to sidle up to him and rub its muzzle on his sleeve. He gave it a little attention, and presently swung his leg into the saddle.

*   *   *

The disillusionment of the federal officer, U.S. Marshal French, took only a few minutes. Bart then started his long journey back to distant Dodge City, in the state of Kansas. Five days later, a little saddle-sore and somewhat out of sorts with himself, he reached the town of Dodge and the headquarters of the Kansas Investigation Company for which he worked.

He found that his boss, Mike Jarrett, was out of town. In his absence, Jarrett's youthful daughter, Michaela, briefed Bart for his next assignment. She also took into safe-keeping his notes on the Roxy Brownwood case which had been compiled in odd minutes during the protracted journey.

For seven days, Bart loaned himself to a livery and freighting company to the north of Dodge which was consistently losing stores between staging points. He had a spot of luck on the third day when he happened upon a couple of thieves breaking out the stores while the freight driver was away with the horses by a creek.

His abrupt appearance provoked sudden gun play, but his nerves were good and his aim accurate. One thief took a bullet wound in the arm, and the other threw down his weapon. Bart appeared back in town with his two prisoners some three hours later.

There, he collected the owner of the freighting company and together they escorted the prisoners to the local lock-up. Bart gave a verbal report to the client and a written resumé of it was prepared for his employer's files.

It was while he was writing up the resumé in his hotel room that a sudden restlessness hit him again. On the freighting job, the great out-of-doors had seemed very desirable following his incarceration in La Junta Prison. He felt that he wanted to change his job for a while, or at least to take up the sort of case which would put him in touch with riding and ranch work.

Perhaps it was that incident in which Jake Harris had been involved which had started him thinking once again about ranching and the fine life under the big sky shared by so many healthy young westerners in the south-west.

★　★　★

Mike Jarrett, the owner of Kansas Investigation Company, was already in his office and working on a backlog of mail when Bart strolled in the next morning. Jarrett was humming to himself, a sure sign that the revenue was coming in and that he was making plenty of money. Jarrett saw Bart's outline through the frosted glass of the partition and called to him.

'Come right on in here, Bart! I didn't expect to see you this early seein' as how you've only jest wrapped up that last assignment.'

Bart did as he was told, placed his hat rather carefully on the hickory limb behind the door and sat himself down in the client's chair. He had his notes on the latest case with him. Leaning forward, he dropped them on the desk top.

'All right, Bart, I'm sure you've made a good summary of the events on the freight line case. As a matter of fact, I met the owner last night and he told me almost all there was to know about it. So I know you did a great job, as usual.'

Jarrett stopped toying with his mail. He ran his right index finger back and forth over his smooth moustache and eyed his man up and down rather pointedly.

'You look a little tired . . . or perhaps jest a trifle bored, then. Take a couple of days off, give yourself a treat, on the firm. I don't want anybody to say I work you to death. Besides, you've been out of town quite a lot lately. Some of your friends will have missed you.'

Bart grinned and nodded. He was about to speak, but Jarrett forestalled him.

'Say, Bart, do you know anybody in Boston, Massachusetts?'

As he said this, Jarrett rose to his feet and crossed the floor on his two long legs to a series of shelves against one wall. Bart reflected that his boss looked very elegant in the English-style riding breeches and black leggings, which were a regular part of his apparel.

'Did you say Boston, Massachusetts?'

Jarrett nodded. He came forward with a small package in his hands. Clearly, he wanted to ask questions about it, but he was denying himself the pleasure. Bart received the parcel from him and belatedly answered the query.

'My mother lives there. I used to live

there myself. What is this in aid of?'

Bart was a bad correspondent. The letters he wrote to his mother did not amount to more than half a dozen a year. She had never sent him a parcel other than at Christmas, or occasionally for his birthday. Latterly, her memory had not been functioning very well and she tended to forget things like birthdays. And now this parcel.

Jarrett gently helped him to his feet. 'Off you go, young fellow. Take a little time off. Go an' examine your parcel at your leisure. I don't want to see you for work till the day after tomorrow. If you want your wages, see Michaela about it.'

Jarrett ushered him through the door before he had been properly thanked. Bart walked like a man in a dream to a coffee house some three doors away down the street. He had a feeling, a premonition, that this small parcel was going to change things for him. And yet, as he reflected upon this feeling, he did not see how that might come about.

Tucked into a remote alcove of the coffee house with a steaming cup in front of him, he opened the parcel and first turned his attention to the letter. It was in two halves. The first half was a kind of diary of everyday events in the life of his mother, now known as Mary Harries.

The second part was the significant one. The writing had suffered in places as though his mother had been under an emotional strain of some sort.

Largely due to the record-keeping side of his job, Bart wrote and read well. His deep-set blue eyes flashed as he read line after line, and slowly began to realise that his premonition might very well be coming true.

His stepfather, Brad Harries, had passed away in his sleep some time earlier in the month. His mother was sorrowing, of course, but she was tough and she was telling her son that she expected to get over it in a relatively short time. Long before this, she had given up trying to lure Bart back to Boston.

Instead, she was recommending him to follow out what his stepfather had in mind for him. Namely, that he should go to Texas, to the Circle H ranch, located at or near a spot called Bonanza Springs, and there make himself known to one Abe Harries, the brother of the deceased.

Quite unexpectedly, Brad Harries had made over to him — Bart — his half share of the Harries estate.

The letter concluded: *I know you've always hankered after making good out West, and now here is your chance. Take the enclosed ring, and make the journey. It was arranged years ago that Brad, or the person he named, should turn up at the ranch with this memento. The other members of the Harries family will honour it. I've written to Abe.*

There was more after that, but most of it was gushing sentimental stuff which the young man skimmed over.

His fingers made heavy going of unwrapping the gold ring with the Circle H embossed upon it. Having laid it bare, he stared at it and toyed with it, his thoughts full of new speculation, while his coffee went cold.

3

The idea of becoming a part of a big Texas ranching outfit quickly grew in Bart's thoughts. Now that the idea was a practical possibility, he knew for sure that it was something he had always wanted. Consequently, he took less than twenty-four hours to present himself at Mike Jarrett's office with his mind made up about the future.

Jarrett was shaken when he knew that his young investigator wanted to quit the firm for good, but he soon saw that Bart's mind was fully made up and after that he did not press him to change it. Jarrett had had plans for Bart. He knew that his daughter, Michaela, a pleasant, intelligent girl who was still under age, had more than a friendly feeling for Bart. Now, however, she would have to get used to the idea of not seeing the young fellow, at least for many months.

Texas was some distance away, and the return journey was not likely to be made in a hurry, even if the person in question decided that after all he could not abide cows all the time. Bart moved out, making brief but friendly farewells, at the end of forty-eight hours after receiving his startling news.

He, too, soon became aware that Texas was some distance away. He jogged south, warmed by thoughts of a settled future in the lone star state, and pleasantly puzzled by the mystery of Jake Harris and the Circle H emblem tattooed on his left hand.

For upwards of two whole weeks, his patient dun quarter horse bore him on his journey. Horse and rider accomplished from ten to fifteen miles each day, and still showed no signs of weakening through over-much effort. They crossed from Kansas into the Indian Strip, which was still a wide, lawless piece of territory for a single traveller to cross unescorted. By careful planning of his day and night periods, Bart avoided the lawless elements, and only paused long enough to pass the time of day with the trail crews which pressed north from the lone star state to northern ranches in Kansas or Wyoming.

On the fifteenth day, he began to see in the distance the gleaming rails of the Texas and California railroad. He had forded Texas' formidable Canadian river during the morning, and now, for the first time, he began to see the railroad as his ally. No sooner had he decided to make use of the railway than he headed his tired horse for the track and sought a good spot from which to wave down the next locomotive to come along.

He was lucky, having no knowledge of timetables, inasmuch as he only had an hour to wait. The conductor came down to the track to talk with him while the dun was run up a ramp and into a horse box. The engineer and fireboy also passed the time of day with him, and upwards of two score passengers showed a polite interest by observing him through the windows or off the observation platform.

He felt quite honoured as the bell, high on the loco, was rung before the train moved on again. Walking through one compartment after another, he was surprised at the relative friendliness of the travellers who preferred to do their journeyings by rail. Several empty seats were indicated and eventually he settled down opposite a man in a dark suit who was gazing absently out of the window, and writing notes on a thick pad in fits and starts.

Bart found a suitable rack for his saddle and other travel items and presently he settled down on a comfortable padded seat and watched the undulating terrain of the Texas Panhandle drift past him. This occupation satisfied him for several hours. The train was doing between fifteen and twenty miles an hour, and soon, instead of feeling sleepy, he began to enthuse about the increased rate of progress towards his destination.

His fellow traveller opposite had taken from his pocket a newspaper which he spread out in front of his face. Thinking that he was entirely unobserved, Bart withdrew the ornate Circle H ring from his finger and held it up to the window so that he could study it with the daylight behind it. Unknown to him, his neighbour had noticed what he was doing.

Bart was so intent upon his study of the ring that he was not aware of the other's interest. He discovered something on that occasion which had escaped him before. Stamped in small capitals on the inside of the ring were two initials. A 'B' and an 'H'. Bart pursed his lips in a soundless whistle. He had not realised before that his own initials were the same as those of the old ex-rancher who had sent him the ring. Brad Harries, the first owner, and now Bart Hall. The same initials, purely by coincidence.

As the passenger opposite started to come out of his newspaper, Bart pushed the ring back on the third finger of his left hand. He was aware that the third finger was the one where married men were likely to wear their rings, but his use of it did not embarrass him. It was just that it fitted him best on that particular finger.

Bart took the opportunity of observing his neighbour. The traveller in question had with him a black leather briefcase bearing the initials H.G.

H.G. was an interesting character. He was about thirty-five years of age, tall, lean and restless with darting bird-like eyes in a slightly pock-marked face with no particular distinguishing features. He wore a well-tailored dark suit, a white shirt and tie and a black cummerbund marked where shirt and trousers met. The gun belt with the single right-handed holster hanging from it started just below the waist band and was partially camouflaged by it.

As though he was too restless to sleep like most of the others in the carriage, H.G. picked up his pad again and started to write things down upon it. He wrote fast, and Bart could only surmise that he was using some form of shorthand.

After a while, Bart got the idea that a railway journey was a good time in which to bring his diary up to date. Since he left Dodge City he had made few entries. Now, with a few hours of enforced leisure, the old habit came back to him. He found that he wanted to bring his personal record up to date. It was no longer any sort of burden, now that his note-making for Jarrett was a thing of the past.

When the ex-investigator started to write, the man sitting opposite appeared to take a marked interest in him for the first time. They exchanged nods, comments about the passing scenery, and — after a time — they smoked together.

'Are you keepin' a diary, friend?' H.G. asked.

Bart coloured up a little. 'Sure, it's jest a matter of personal jottings. Only, now, after a long journey on horseback I find I'm gettin' some pleasure out of it. Could I ask what you are so interested in writing?'

The other preceded his answer with a relaxed but dry-sounding laugh. 'My name is Homer Grayson. I work as a journalist for a newspaper in Fort Worth. The paper is called the *Clarion*. I guess scribbling on a pad is second nature to me.'

Bart said: 'Howdy, I'm Bart Hall, on my way to join a ranch further south. I'm glad to make your acquaintance, Homer. As a matter of fact, this is probably my first long trip on a train. I'm usin' it to cut down on my travellin' time to Bonanza Springs.'

Grayson put aside his pad and warmed in his attitude. He did not ask any very searching questions, but Bart found himself telling little things about himself and his start in life up the east coast, prior to moving west. Grayson showed himself to be a good listener, and when Bart dried up on occasion because he did not want to reveal too much to a complete stranger, the newspaper-man covered his embarrassment by talking about his job and the kind of work he liked best.

Bart found himself learning about journalism in general, and about free-lancing in particular. The ex-detective was intrigued to find that there were newspaper proprietors who would pay a good reporter to travel and pick up good copy for his newspaper, and that the same reporter had the right to offer some of his work to other papers in other towns.

A few shots of whisky from Grayson's flask, and the gentle jogging of the train's motion across the state, helped to loosen tongues quite a bit more, and when the great woodburner pulled into a town called Farewell, the last town on the Texas side of the border with New Mexico territory, it seemed quite a natural thing to do for the two travellers to disembark together and seek out the same hotel.

After a good meal, they played a few hands at poker before retiring to Bart's room with a half-full whisky bottle and two tumblers. For upwards of another hour they talked and drank and smoked, while all the time the sound of merry-making carried up to them from the saloon below.

Once, when the singing was excessively noisy, Grayson remarked on it. 'I guess there's a kind of cosiness in a nice dry hotel bedroom without anything to bother about except what time the drinkers are goin' to turn in. For me, though, sleepin' out in good weather round a camp fire has a certain attraction.

'For one thing, the singin' always seems more tuneful and the tired cowhands are friendlier. I can see all the faces of the boys I was with round jest such a camp fire only three nights ago.'

'You mean your work takes you into

touch with the trail crews?' Bart queried, as he shifted his position on top of the bedclothes.

'Why sure, Bart, newspapers and newsmen are interested in jest about everything. Why, I've been interviewin' trail crews for several weeks now, jest to be able to tell the *Clarion*'s readers what it feels like to be one of a team drivin' Texas longhorns to the markets further north.'

'I've done the same thing. Met up with trail crews, I mean.' Bart was so interested that he wagged a finger in Grayson's direction. 'I want to ask you something. In your travels, have you ever come across a ranch called the Circle H? Or a crew drovin' cattle from such a ranch? It's located quite near to a town called Bonanza Springs.'

Grayson pushed his hat forward. Slowly, he shook his head. He had no clear recollection of having had any specific contact with the Circle H, but he certainly was interested. Bart, who was rendered quite loquacious by the excellent whisky, had revealed quite a bit about the two founders of the Circle H and the rings which they possessed before it occurred to him that he was saying a lot more than was necessary.

As soon as he had the idea that he was being incautious, he feigned weariness, and Grayson at once got up to take his leave.

'One more thing, other than to thank you,' the journalist murmured, 'I'm travellin' south at a fairly early hour tomorrow. On horseback. If I haven't bored you with my conversation today, I'd take it as a privilege if we could ride together.'

Bart grinned. He shook hands on the new arrangement, and at once flopped into bed. Before he dropped off to sleep, he worked out one or two more useful sentences for his diary, but his eyes were shutting before he could get around to writing them up.

★ ★ ★

From Farewell, the route was south for both travellers.

One hundred miles of undulating trails mostly at altitudes of three to six thousand feet. The horses of both men had improved through the rest they had had on board the train, and, consequently, they were both still full of stamina when the riding companions arrived in the town of Lubbock, the last stop before they parted.

Seven days of jogging along on horseback, side by side with another man, makes for quick friendship. It formed a basis for more exchanges between the two, and by the time Lubbock came up Homer Grayson had a pretty fair idea of what lay ahead of Bart.

They ate a rather sumptuous meal in a big restaurant on the evening of their arrival, and talked of their respective journeys after they had parted.

'Reckon I'll take the stage for the next day or two, jest to give my horse a rest,' Bart decided as the food came to an end. 'Maybe another six days is all I need to come up with Bonanza Springs and the Circle H. How'll it be with you?'

Homer chuckled good-humouredly. 'Oh, my base, Fort Worth, is twice as far away as you want to go. I'll take my time. This is a good place for sendin' off some of my work by telegraph. I want to get something worthwhile in front of my boss before he sees my homely face.'

The two laughed heartily. They drank quite a quantity of beer before turning in, and Homer was outside the hotel and mail office the following morning to give Bart a shake of the hand and wave him on his way.

Of the various modes of travel, Bart found stagecoach journeying the least desirable, but he contrived several useful short spells of sleep, in spite of the endless bumping up and down on the leather straps. For two whole days he used the stage with its six-horse team. And that was all the time he felt he could give to the uncomfortable conveyance.

In the last settlement of any size before Bonanza Springs, a cowtown called Woodford, he finally parted company with the overland coach and determined to make the rest of the journey on horseback, as most ranch-minded men would expect him to do.

He booked a room in the Ford Hotel, a two-storey establishment on Central Street, and, having deposited his gear, he turned his attention to food and gradually worked to replace the energy he had lost, and also to slake his thirst. He was missing Homer Grayson already, although at times he had thought that Homer had a mighty curiosity, even for a newspaper reporter.

At a comparatively early hour, he retired to his room on the first floor with a small flat bottle of whisky and three short cigars. Even then he still had thirty or forty dollars left out of the wages which Jarrett had paid him. He was beginning to think that he had managed his protracted five-hundred-mile journey quite economically.

There were two single beds in the room. He tested each of them and decided that the one further from the door was the more to his liking. Having made up his mind to use it, he then partially stripped off and began to pace up and down, his mind racing with excitement again now that his destination was so close.

He wondered how Abe Harries would greet him. If, as his mother had said, Harries acknowledged the ring which had been Brad's, he might even then have doubts about taking on a young man as his partner whose main experience in life had very little to do with cows.

It was a sobering thought, one which sent Bart to his bed with the half-bottle intact and the cigars unsmoked. About a half-hour later sleep claimed him. It rejected him again when a slight noise disturbed his slumbers. He had locked the door of his room and dumped the key on a chest of drawers. So much flashed through his brain even before he opened his eyes.

He blinked himself awake in the faint light of the moon, cautiously turned his head to look across and beyond the empty bed, and saw the bent back of an intruder who was crouched over the chest of drawers. The fellow had on a dark suit and a big stetson with a wide brim.

Bart did not wait to discover more. His thoughts were on the rest of his savings, which had been tucked away in one of those drawers. Without waiting to find his gun, he squirmed out of bed, dived across the second unoccupied bed and caught the intruder around the waist.

The unknown man made an angry noise and turned sharply. The impetus of Bart's trajectory made him lose his grip on the other's waist. He recovered quickly and came up from the floor as a square-toed black riding boot was aimed at his head. He avoided the kick, taking the boot toe on the side of his shoulder.

In rising swiftly, he again caught his man unprepared, and this time he threw a great haymaking swing at the shadowy features. His aim was good and his luck in, for the moment. He felt the Circle H ring connect hard with flesh and bone. The knowledge that he had probably marked the thief gave him a brief flash of satisfaction.

The intruder sailed backwards, losing his hat. Bart followed up closely, determined to safeguard his few possessions whatever happened. Just as he was bending over the fallen man, however, something which hurt and sent his senses reeling connected with the side of his head.

As he slumped, with all manner of bright lights shooting through his head, he realised that there must have been another man in the room. A man he had not seen at all. He also realised that what had hit him was not a fist, but a missile of some sort, and that was all . . .

4

Bart could not tell at first how many minutes had elapsed since his senses left him. When he started to think constructively, he was still seeing occasional bright lights in his skull. By comparison, the faint light of the moon through the room window was almost non-existent.

At first he was annoyed at finding himself on the wrong bed. The initial annoyance gave way to a much greater one when he recollected how some weapon or some thrown object had connected with his temple. His head was swollen and he could feel the blood pounding through that part of it.

In a flash he remembered the other details and then he was noticing the small aches in his wrists, his ankles and his back. Strips of rawhide had been attached to his limbs, and in order to delay him a little longer the ankle cord had been connected to the wrist cord by a short connecting length which kept his back bent.

As he wriggled and nibbled at the gag in his mouth he found that he was almost in the shape of a question mark. To his surprise he found that the gun belt was exactly where he had left it. But the gun was of no use, except perhaps in a dire emergency to attract attention.

There was no sign of a knife in the small sheath attached to the same belt. Bart began to feel excessively annoyed. He rolled off the bed on to the floor and tested the strength of the connecting strip of rawhide. It was weaker than he had thought. By straining at it for a minute or two he managed to burst it and so contrived to straighten his back and assume his normal shape.

The gag was rather tightly tied about his mouth. He was tasting blood from the corners of it by the time he contrived to force the gag down over his neck. For upwards of a couple of minutes after that he worked to regain his breath. To quicken his revival he hopped on his tethered ankles to the window, which was open, and there sucked in great mouthfuls of air.

As his lungs expanded, for a few seconds he thought of bellowing out into the street and disturbing the populace. But that would have been unfair. A robbery was not so rare an occurrence that everyone should be disturbed.

All the same, he ought to alert somebody, otherwise the man or men who had been in his room would get clear of town without difficulty. He checked in one or two places, including under the bed, for his knife and failed to find it. The next best thing was to get down below and turn out one of the servants. Once the cords were off him he would be able to think more clearly and devise a plan of some sort.

He hopped to the door and then realised that he was in his underwear. If any of the ladies staying in the hotel saw him like that they would almost certainly complain. Still fuming inwardly, he snatched a blanket off the nearest bed and wrapped it around him. In that cocoon-like garb he opened the door of the room and hopped out on to the landing.

Reaching the head of the stairs presented no particular problem with a low light burning in the nearest lamp, but as he started the descent, still hopping, he caught his heels on the back of a step and lost his balance. An over-developed sense of propriety made him hold on to the blanket wrapped around him when he could have put his trussed hands to good use.

His back connected with several steps. Half-way down he rolled and cracked the uninjured side of his head against the wall. That brought an involuntary groan from him. A few seconds of dizziness were sufficient to start him on the second part of the descent, and it was while he was involved in that, at times head over heels, that the blanket parted from him and revealed him, as the intruders had left him, in his underwear.

His shoulder connected with a post at the foot of the stairs and that provoked a couple of round oaths. Poor Bart ended up on knees and elbows with his head throbbing and his self-restraint all gone.

'Can't somebody give me a bit of help, for goodness' sake?' he bellowed in a loud voice.

One call was enough, following the string of thuds which marked the descent. A servant of the hotel, a tall man in a slack-fitting gown, came from the rear corridor, but hung back instead of stepping smartly forward to give assistance.

Bart moved slowly to his feet like a prize fighter who had taken a count. A stout woman, peering down from the head of the stairs, saw him at that moment. She let out an unearthly scream, and drew from Bart his most fiendish expression to date.

He shook his tethered wrists in the servant's face. 'For Pete's sake, mister, can't you see I'm in trouble, that your hotel has been robbed? Get a knife, *muy pronto*!'

The servant hesitated, collided with another man, a barman, and finally went away to get the knife. Two minutes later, Bart was freed of his bonds and massaging his aching ankles and wrists. The barman stayed beside Bart, seated on the carpet at the foot of the stairs. He rolled smokes for the two of them while the other man hastily changed his apparel and went looking for the peace officer.

Safely wrapped inside his blanket, and drawing on the soothing smoke, Bart regarded the tousled cluster of onlookers above him.

'If I were you, folks, I'd get back into your rooms an' lock the doors. I've been hit on the head an' robbed. Don't go off to sleep yet, though, because the town marshal will probably come along, an' he may want to search the hotel.'

The stout woman was the first to go away. Two men hovered for a minute longer, but the sound of heavy boots coming down the boards of the sidewalk prompted them to do as Bart had suggested. As the town marshal came in through the foyer, Bart and the barman rose slowly to their feet.

'What in tarnation has been goin' on here? This here is a peaceful town. I don't know how long it is since I was last roused out of bed. What's been happenin'?'

'If you'd care to stop talkin' an' listen for a change, Marshal, I'll be glad to tell you. You'd better come up to my room.'

Marshal Pete Luckett, a lean panther of a man, nearing fifty in age, regarded Bart with an outraged look in his smouldering bulbous eyes. He had a shotgun under his arm and the appropriate star pinned to the left side of a fringed jacket. His hat was shapeless, and his hollow cheeks deeply lined behind a drooping grey moustache which had been singed by cigarettes.

'If you're wantin' my co-operation, mister, you'd best keep a civil tongue in your head. I don't like strangers at the best of times, especially I don't like those who give me work at inconvenient hours.'

'Are you sayin' you only keep the peace when the time is convenient, Marshal? Or have I misjudged you? The folks in this hotel are not all strangers. Right now, they're lookin' for protection of some sort from you. I hope you ain't up for election in the near future.'

The two workers gasped at the way in which Bart addressed the marshal, but the affronted young man did not wait to see the effect of his words. Instead, he went off up the stairs, leaving the other to follow.

They met again, face to face, in the doorway of Bart's room. The later had half a mind to apologise and start again, but his limbs and his temple were throbbing and the smouldering look in the peace officer's eyes killed his inclination to improve the situation.

'I awoke about a half-hour ago, I suppose. In the far bed. I tackled a man in a dark suit who was rootin' about in that chest of drawers. I was doin' quite well for a man so soon out of a deep sleep, but there must have been another man in the room. One I hadn't reckoned on. He could have been standin' in that alcove.'

He pointed to the spot in question beyond the second bed.

'Something thrown hit me on the temple and that was that.'

Marshal Luckett swallowed his indignation and prowled the room. At the same time, Bart went through the drawers after lighting a lamp and turning it well up. For the first time he was giving his full attention to the matter of the theft, and his pulse was racing all over again as he came to an inevitable conclusion. The balance of his money, the small wad left in the drawer, was still there. He searched his pockets and his saddle pockets, too.

Presently, Luckett stood before him, radiating hostility. The bulbous eyes noted the wad of notes which Bart held before him.

'Well, mister. What did your two intruders steal from you?'

It was while Bart was holding the paper money in his nervous fingers that he began to be aware of the real theft. His ring, the one which he had received back in Dodge City, was no longer on his finger.

'Give me another minute, Marshal,' he murmured.

Marshal Luckett sat down rather heavily on the nearer of the two beds and lowered his shotgun. He began to whistle tunelessly while Bart went over everything again. Bart's face was tense again now, his hurts temporarily forgotten. If the sole purpose of the intrusion had been to steal his ring, then the thief must have been someone who knew who he was, and where he was going, and for what purpose. And that, surely, narrowed down the field a bit.

Luckett whistled on, apparently unimpressed when Bart pulled out all the drawers, one at a time, and peered behind them. At this stage, the ex-detective did not expect to find his ring. He was looking for another item; one which perhaps tied in with the other.

At last, he had to admit that he was baffled. His diary was also missing! His personal record of things done and things observed. Anyone with the diary in their possession would know a great deal about the diarist.

Bart began to perspire as he considered what he was up against, but he was mindful of the unfriendly peace officer who wanted to know more of his business. Fortunately, at that moment, the young man's inborn tact saved the situation. He picked up the flat whisky bottle and put it into the marshal's hands.

'Go on,' he urged, 'break it open an'

take a good swig. You deserve it.'

If anything could thaw out Pete Luckett on a night operation it was good whisky, and this bottle contained as good a brew as could be obtained anywhere in Woodford. The marshal peered into Bart's face, as though seeking confirmation for the suggestion. Bart nodded. The peace officer bit through the fastening at the top of the bottle and drew out the cork with his teeth. He nodded in a civil fashion before putting the neck of the bottle to his lips.

Bart straightened up and leaned against the nearest wall, watching his guest's Adam's apple bobbing up and down as he drank. Luckett was giving himself a generous measure, but Bart did not mind. He was a stranger, and he needed co-operation.

Suddenly he knew what had to be done. He started to pull on his shirt. His pants followed. By the time he was hauling on his boots Luckett had gone past the stage where he could protest a thirst.

'So tell me again what you lost.'

Bart had not made any statement this far, but he made up for his earlier reticence. 'No money, but a very personal ring and a private diary. The thief must have known a lot about me and my personal affairs. I can tell you in confidence that that ring is the key to a fortune. If you think it's all right, we could look around the empty rooms of the hotel, and maybe do a tour of the liveries. You see, the thief had to be known to me. That much is clear. If I saw a familiar face around town, I wouldn't have to look any further.'

Luckett accepted a cigar. He crackled it between his finger and thumb. Lubricated with whisky, he was not averse to doing the rounds of the town, but the way he rolled his bulbous eyes showed that he had little hope of finding the wrong-doer.

Bart completed his dressing and side by side they moved down to the lower floor. Bart surreptitiously massaged his ring finger. Prior to the discovery of the ring's loss he had associated the pain in his finger with being trussed up. Now, he realised that the ring must have been wrenched clear with some force. His knuckle was bruised.

One or two cautious heads watched the pair on the stairs, but the curious ones withdrew almost at once. They checked the lower level, back and front, and made a slow tour of the main thoroughfares, which were not very numerous. The only signs of life amounted to a card school of four well-known characters in an otherwise unoccupied saloon.

Fifteen minutes later they parted. Bart shook hands with Luckett and thanked him for his vigilance. He bestowed the rest of the whisky on the official and promised to visit his office fairly early in the morning.

After they had parted, Bart walked the boards again, checking at each of the livery stables that there was no sign of light or life. The time came, however, when his pains began to play him up and he had to admit to himself that he was overtired.

He bathed his head on his return to the hotel and did what he could to make himself comfortable. Thoughts of his loss, however, kept him from sound sleep.

In the morning he visited the peace office before indulging in food. Luckett was much more agreeable in the daytime. He did more searching and pandered to Bart's small demands, but there were no signs of likely strangers. Nor had anyone noted a hasty departure.

Bart's hopes were based upon the discovery of a man with a new wound upon his face; a wound which might have a ring and a letter H imprinted on it. No such person was discovered. No one had been to see the doctor with such an injury.

The ring and the diary had vanished and the thief, or thieves, along with them. Bart broke off the search, thanked the marshal again, and sauntered into the nearest café. His interest and enthusiasm for the future had been dashed. As he waited for his food to be cooked, he wondered if there was any sense in going on to the Circle H.

5

By that same evening, Bart was still feeling frustrated and uncertain of himself. He prowled the bars for upwards of two hours, thinking over his circumstances in life and striving hard to come to some sort of a conclusion.

In each of the bars he enjoyed the beer and the other drinkers permitted him to be solitary as he leaned on the counter. He saw the other clients and yet their presence had no impact upon him.

To work out the future he analysed the past. He had been due for a move, or a change of some sort, from his regular occupation in Dodge. One thing he could not bring himself to do now and that was to backtrack to Kansas and admit to Mike Jarrett that he had lost his credentials. He was still young enough and impressionable enough to want to avoid looking foolish in the eyes of a former employer.

As the beer and the passage of time calmed him, he found that he was curious about the Circle H cow ranch and its present owner, Abe Harries. He wondered if the old man ran the ranch with some sort of military discipline, or whether he had sons who did the work for him. After all, Abe must be getting on in years, and if he was well off he might well delegate his duties to others.

Bart's interest in the ranch and the family went deeper than he had at first thought. Coupled with this basic interest was his own wish to have a part in the ranch work, to share the responsibility and to acquire some of the skills peculiar to a cowman.

Long before he came to a decision about what to do, subconsciously his mind was made up for him.

The robbery had hurt his pride. He had been caught napping, and that had not pleased him. Probably due to his own foolishness some man had taken an unhealthy interest in his personal affairs. If he had talked too much, the only man he could think of who might be behind the robbery was Homer Grayson, the newspaper man.

Bart had come up against many kinds of criminal types. If he had been taken in by Grayson, if Grayson was not a newspaper reporter at all, then he had to be a confidence trickster, one who 'conned' others out of their money or their belongings.

Such a possibility made Bart's pulse quicken, but he had to envisage such a possibility. No one had had access to his diary, for instance, since Dodge, other than Grayson, who might have seen it on occasion when they were travelling together on horseback. In fact, he might have possibly laid hands on it during those nights spent out in the open between Farewell and Lubbock.

Bart controlled his anger and tried to reason things out some more. No one would steal the ring just for its value in gold. Coupled with the diary, it was the key to a fortune. Someone would have to go along to the Circle H and present himself as the heir of Brad Harries, deceased.

And that consideration was where Bart started to drink more deeply. An impostor would appear at the ranch and masquerade as himself — if the diary was to be utilised. And that was a thing he could not allow to happen.

If he went along openly to the Circle H and told who he was, he could expect that they would not believe him, but he might be able to stay around long enough to confound the man who went along to acquire his inheritance, and that would give him some satisfaction, even if it was only that felt through revenge.

★ ★ ★

After another spell of travel on horseback similar in duration to that which had brought him from Lubbock

to Woodford, Bart rode into the town of
Bonanza Springs at ten o'clock one
morning. He headed his steaming
mount directly for the hitch rail outside
the peace office on Main.

The shingle outside the office bore the
name of the man he was anxious to see.
*Marshal Lobo Farnes, Town Marshal,
Bonanza Springs*. Underneath the board,
scratched out on the ancient paintwork,
someone had inscribed another message.
*Any hombre who don't believe this step
inside and get confirmation.*

Bart hitched the dun, slackened off
the saddle and stepped inside the
building with a bleak smile upon his
face. He had in his hand a small scrap
of paper written out for him by Pete
Luckett, a man who had improved on
acquaintance.

The bulky fellow filling the swivel
chair behind the desk was wearing the
marshal's badge. He turned to face the
newcomer, screwed up his swarthy face
and gave a spiky-toothed grin which
might or might not have been the

reason for his nickname.

'What can I do for you, mister?'

A touch of devilment made Bart fold the note into the shape of a paper dart. He aimed it at the desk and the marshal caught it, rumbling good-humouredly. His short, strong fingers straightened out the paper and he read what was on it.

The brief interlude gave Bart a chance to study the peace officer. Farnes looked naturally aggressive, which was probably an asset in his line of business. In his early forties, he was of average height, but overweight. Tufts of crisp brown hair stuck out of his checked shirt near the neck. He had a luxurious moustache and stiff bristly hair of the same texture.

Farnes rocked himself back and forth in the chair. He breathed out rather noisily. 'Okay, so you're Bart Hall, a buddy of Pete Luckett. Howdy. What can I do for you?'

Bart gestured towards an upright chair, received a nod and sat down upon it. 'I'm glad to meet you, Marshal. Right now I'm on my way to the Circle H. Back in Woodford I had trouble. My hotel room was broken into and I lost two important items. They were my credentials. I've come from much further afield, in fact. From Dodge City, Kansas.'

Farnes nodded slowly, at the same time giving his wide sweep of moustache a lift. 'You have more to tell,' he prompted.

Bart nodded and pushed back his hat. 'If you know anything of the Harries family you'd know one of them them left this territory and settled on the east coast. A man named Brad. Brad married my mother, and that, in a roundabout sort of way, is why I am here. Brad Harries died a short while back, an' he nominated me as his heir.'

At last, personal curiosity showed itself in the face of the hirsute marshal. 'Is that so? Well now, I don't rightly think the Harries on the ranch know anything about that. Not that they would go out of their way to tell me, of course. But you said a while ago that you had lost your credentials. Do Abe Harries and his boys actually know you?'

Bart gave a wry smile. His restlessness made him stand up and straddle the chair he was using. 'That's the crux of my problem, Marshal. They don't know me. With the stolen items an impostor will almost certainly turn up and pass himself off as me. But I can't take that lyin' down.

'What I need is to get close to the Harries family before the impostor has a chance to go into action. I have to talk to somebody, gain the family's confidence, if I can, without my credentials. It won't be easy, especially as I don't know the family an' they don't know me.'

The young visitor stopped talking. He felt automatically for his tobacco sack and gently rocked himself back and forth on the upright chair which creaked slightly. Farnes produced a match for the pair of them. Clearly he was interested in Bart's story, but he was cautious and he waited for more revelations.

'Am I right in thinkin' that Abe Harries is still active an' fit, an' givin' the orders on the ranch?'

Farnes blew out smoke, watched it ascend in the dusty atmosphere of the room, and finally nodded. 'Yer, Abe is still around, all right, but he doesn't do all the ram-roddin'. He has his two boys actively engaged in the runnin' of the spread. If you wanted to talk to the boss, you'd have to seek out Abe, an' that's for sure.'

'Tell me, is there any possible chance of gettin' in touch with Abe, apart from in his own house? Does he come into town regularly, or anything like that?'

Bart's face had assumed the brooding look. He studied the peace officer's expression with his straight dark brows almost joined over the pale blue eyes.

'Nope. His movements are irregular in that respect. All I can suggest, seein' as how time seems to be against you, is that you try an' make your way on to Circle H territory without upsettin' the regular hands, an' aim to talk with the old man. But that ain't goin' to be easy.'

'Is there any special reason why I can't ride all the way up to the buildings?'

'Yer, I guess there is. You see, the Circle H is a pretty extensive cattle outfit. They have three distinct regions on which to run their cattle. Their herds take a lot of watchin'. In the past year they have lost a lot of cattle in small bunches through rustlin'.

'That's why it ain't easy for a stranger to make his way up to the house. The cowpunchers are trained to be mighty mean, an' they drive off anybody who don't seem to have the right to be there.'

Farnes stopped talking rather abruptly, and Bart blinked at him wondering what he had in mind. He had a feeling that the peace officer had a suggestion of some sort to make, and he was right.

The marshal wagged a whiskery finger at him.

'Now, see here, Bart, you could be spinnin' me the father an' mother of a yarn over Brad Harries' death and all, but I'm goin' to take a chance on you. There is a way in which a careful man could work his way on to Circle H territory, an' I'm goin' to outline the route to you. Of course, you'll realise that in the future jest because I believe what you've told me you can't expect everybody to take you at face value.'

Bart accepted the marshal's view of the situation. He said as much and expressed himself grateful for the information given.

★　★　★

The widespread acreage of the Circle H was usually well watered because it was located in a shallow valley which tended to trap moisture. Apart from the falling rain, it had its own permanent supply of water within the banks of a stream known as Brothers' Creek. This watercourse skirted the west side of north range and home range and also formed the boundary along that aspect.

Bart Hall was not likely to see Brothers' Creek on his first penetration of Circle H land because he was heading into it from the north-east. Most people who had business with the thriving ranch left Bonanza on a semi-permanent track which meandered gradually south-west until it crossed the Circle H boundary line about three miles from town.

Bart headed first of all to westward out of town. Inside two miles he first set eyes upon a gully, a dried-out watercourse which Marshal Farnes had mentioned. This gully had once been the bed and course of a promising stream, but at some time earlier in the century geographical and geological changes in the area had caused the stream to dry up along most of its length.

The *arroyo* provided a means of access to Circle H land, but the owners did not bother too much about the undesirable accessibility because at one point along its length a rock-slip of rather alarming proportions had cascaded rocks and boulders of all shapes and sizes into the old bed and made it a very unlikely route for running out cattle. Rustlers had at times feasted off stolen Circle H beeves, but the *arroyo* had never been used as a route for spiriting away the stock.

Bart made his way along the *arroyo* with his head full of conflicting thoughts. He knew that for the first time in his life he was actually moving over Circle H land and that if his luck held he might one day own a vast proportion of it, and of the cattle which roamed and fed upon it.

He could see that the Harries were likely to be hostile to a stranger who came along and declared himself to be the heir of their kin. He would have a devilish job to convince them that he was genuine, especially since he had never spent a lot of time in Brad Harries' company.

His thoughts took a change of topic when he came to the spot where the rocks had fallen from the higher of the two upthrusts of outcrop on the north side. He wondered what subterranean heat had been sufficient to cause the collapse of the majestic heap and when it had occurred.

Presently, the high-stepping dun had cleared the stony area and the arroyo had taken a slight turn in direction. On either hand robust patches of lush bunch grass swayed in the slight breeze of the early afternoon. He tried to see the vegetation from the point of view of a rancher. With no experience, he knew how valuable that sort of grass was for animal fodder. In a way, he was disappointed at this stage because he had not already encountered the bawling of healthy cattle.

At this stage he began to feel sleepy.

The heat appeared to be hanging in the sky. He tried to think how far along this remote watercourse the first signs of ranch life would be. Would it be cattle on the hoof, or men on horseback? The grasses sighed in the breeze. Instead of feeling more comfortable in that situation, the soughing noise added to his drowsiness, and without knowing quite when it occurred he slipped into a light sleep.

The dun must have been aware of it. It kept on, following the obvious route, and upwards of fifteen minutes went by during which the terrain was always slightly downhill. A pleasant shadow, that afforded by a ragged cluster of waterside trees, was edging steadily nearer to the dozing rider by the time that he roused himself again.

Bart found to his surprise that there was water ahead of him. At a particularly low level of the *arroyo* a small permanent lake had formed, supporting willows, pines and occasional oaks along its extensive length. The slight sounds which birds make over water had been the ones to rouse him.

The dun, as soon as he had roused himself, increased its pace, and did not slow up again until its feet were all in shallow water. Bart pushed back his flat-crowned hat and flapped his grey jacket against his body. He was dabbing his face and forehead with a pale blue bandanna when he received an unmistakable warning that he was not alone.

It all seemed to happen at once. The great boom of the gun came rattling down the surface of the water. The branch of the pine above Bart's head was severed with a crack like lightning. It fell just wide of him, brushing his shoulder as it dropped into the water with a resounding splash.

Someone was challenging his right to be where he was.

The horse's reaction came a second or two later, but it was just as devastating. It pranced up on its hind legs, in an attitude which was rare in its career, and before Bart could recover from the string of simultaneous surprises, he had slipped over the animal's rump and dropped into the cooling waters of the lake.

6

There was no mistaking the kind of weapon which had been fired to sever the tree branch. It was a shoulder gun of heavy calibre. A Sharps buffalo gun. The sort of weapon which kicks the shoulder of the firer really hard when it is fired.

All this Bart understood as he floundered in the shallow water and wondered what his fate was going to be. The startled dun made off to one side, scrambling out of the water and gradually recovering some of its poise and calm amid the trees on the eastern side.

The man who had discharged the weapon was some distance away down one of the banks of the lake. That was another thing about the Sharps. It could be fired with remarkable accuracy at relatively long distances. But to pick off a man in the position which Bart was in the gun had to be fired from comparatively near at hand.

Bart calmed quickly. If he was to die by the next shot from the powerful weapon there was nothing he could do about it. He was not going to plead with his unknown assailant. His first bit of reasoning had to do with the type of person who had fired at him. Was it a member of the ranching family or someone acting on the owner's behalf? Or was it possibly some other interloper who sought to frighten him off?

He discarded the second theory because the discharge of the weapon had been such a loud one. Anyone using a Sharps when not observed was throwing away the chance of remaining undiscovered. Obviously, the gunman was a Harries, or someone acting for the boss.

He stood up and called: 'Hey, you there! Will you show yourself?'

His voice made an echo of sorts down the banks of the lake, but no one broke cover, and no one attempted to answer him. He was to receive no sort of help in his attempt to make a proper contact with the buffalo gunner. That being so, he felt that the maximum amount of caution was the only thing that was going to get him anywhere.

He had two courses of action. One was to make a sudden plunge sideways in an effort to gain the shelter of the trees, and the other was to walk forward through the shallows towards the place where his assailant was hidden. His urge was to try for shelter, but his reason counselled otherwise. If his move for the trees was interpreted wrongly, he might end his days in that cool, pleasant water, having stopped the second shot.

Sighing to himself, he started to walk forward. He wanted to observe every inch of leafy cover on either hand ahead of him, but he did not have the chance because the bottom of the lake was uneven in depth and the bank undulated, too. He had to keep looking down, and perhaps that was the best thing to do.

His boots were apparently tightening against his limbs when he heard the ominous click of the gun hammer some sixty yards further down the lake. The sound chilled his blood, or seemed to do so. He stopped where he was and raised his hands wide of his shoulders in case the unknown man got the wrong impression.

He licked his lips well to keep them moist, and when no challenge rang out, he moved on again. On the east side a narrow spit of land went by, a tiny peninsula, and beyond it in the cove which followed he saw the business end of the buffalo gun and the determined veteran who was holding it.

The appearance and pose of the gunman was almost as arresting as the threat of the gun. Even behind the bulky weapon it was possible to see much of him. He was around sixty in age, a stony-eyed man with a thin lined face. His brows were curling and his over-long iron-grey sideburns had the effect of broadening his visage. His face was foreshortened by a crumpled red bandanna around the chin and a large brimmed grey stetson which was dented at the front.

Bart nodded. 'What does a man have to do to stop another hombre menacin' him with a buffalo gun?'

He stood there, lightly poised on his feet in the shallow water and waited for an answer.

'Trespassin' is considered to be a serious crime in some parts of this county, stranger. Right now, I ain't made up my mind whether you should be ventilated properly with this here popgun, so I'd take it as a kindly act if you'd move over to the bank a little way lower down, an' keep your hands in sight.'

Bart nodded. He waded past the man and the gun, and it was only when he was stepping ashore that the instruction to toss aside his weapon came. He threw his Colt to a spot half-way between the gunman and himself. After that, he slowly lowered himself to the ground and started to wring out his clothing.

'Did Abe Harries say you had to turn that buffalo gun on anyone you didn't know?'

The veteran gave a wry chuckle. 'It might surprise you to know that I am Abe Harries, young fellow, an' I don't have the habit of talking to myself. What brought you on to my property?'

Bart went on with his drying chores, but when he talked he thought about what he was going to say with great care. 'My stepfather, your brother, died a few weeks back.'

'How's that again?'

The rancher had laid aside his weapon by this time. His voice betrayed a sharp interest. Bart let him mull over what had already been said for a minute before answering.

'Your brother, Brad Harries, the one who went to live in Boston. He died, I was sayin'. My mother is his widow. My mother sent to me at my place of work, in Kansas, a letter and a ring. The ring bore a certain device on it, one known to you. A capital letter 'H' and a circle. That made me Brad's heir. But I don't have the ring now because it was stolen from me jest a short while ago in the town of Woodford.

'That's why I'm here. I couldn't allow myself to drop out of the runnin' without sayin' what happened. Brad was a little bit taller than you are.'

Bart finished wringing out his clothes. He hung his jacket on a bush and flapped his pants in the slight breeze. Abe bit a huge lump off a piece of chewing tobacco. From time to time the older man shot covert glances at the newcomer.

'How do I know you ain't an impostor? Some fellow who maybe overheard a conversation about the Harries an' the ring which Brad had?'

Bart moved closer, talking earnestly. 'You don't, but I can assure you that the real impostor will turn up with that ring. He might arrive any time. He'll tell a good tale, too, because he stole my personal diary. I don't expect you to believe me, but I'd like the chance to stay around for a while. Maybe you could take me on as an ordinary hand?'

Abe asked a few questions in a half-hearted fashion, but at length he agreed to Bart's suggestion. About a half-hour after they had first met, they moved away from the lake in the general direction of the home buildings.

* * *

Bart counted seven buildings as well as a couple of small sheds when the Circle H headquarters came in sight. He was taken to the bunkhouse and given a bunk, and then he visited the cookhouse next and was given coffee and a light meal.

After he had sorted out his few belongings and spread himself on his bunk, he talked about things of no consequence for nearly half an hour with the cook, Ah Fong, and the blacksmith, Dick Wood. All the time he was talking, uppermost in his mind was the meeting with the regular cowpunchers who were still away on the east range. They, he felt sure, would soon see that he was a beginner at their sort of work. He wondered if they would accept him quite readily or not.

Bart was surprised when Abe came to the bunkhouse door and called for him by name. He turned on his side and came to his feet.

'Was there something you wanted, Mr Harries?'

Abe nodded, scratched his head and waited impatiently for Bart to step outside the building. Out in the open, the young man saw for the first time Abe's two sons, Ike and Red. Ike was the older, a big-jawed, taciturn individual with sketchy eyebrows and thinning dark brown hair under a heavy stetson rolled Texas-style.

Ike was in his middle thirties. His brother, Red, so called because of the carrotty colour of his hair, was twenty-seven and the more talkative of the two. Red had rather bold grey eyes under sparse brows set in a broad cleanshaven face.

Abe said hesitantly: 'Boys, this here is Bart Hall, the fellow I told you about, and you'll want to get better acquainted.'

The rancher gave Bart a peculiar sort of look, turned on his heel and went off around the house as though he had something very important on his mind. Bart blinked after him, but did not allow the old man's departure to rattle him. He beamed at the two brothers, and extended his hand towards Ike, the older.

'I'm pleased to meet you, Ike. I've heard your uncle talk about you.'

Ike Harries appeared not to notice the extended hand. Instead, he turned away and shrugged his thick, sloping shoulders. Bart's puzzled glance then fell upon Red, the younger of the two. He whipped off his stetson, cleared his throat rather noisily and gave a casual nod.

'Like Pa said, we'd like to get better acquainted.'

Bart almost blurted out that they were not showing any special interest in furthering their acquaintance with him, but he managed to restrain himself. Meanwhile, Red muttered something and indicated that Bart was to follow them. They walked off, around the house, a yard gap between them, and he followed, wondering how he was going to break through their reserve to achieve any sort of *rapport*.

The Harries brothers led the way to the further of the two stables. Ike glanced back over his shoulder and then stepped inside. Red side-stepped and permitted Bart to go in first. The young investigator was full of curiosity about this pair of brothers and the coming interview. It almost seemed as if they were intent upon showing him some of the spread's best horses.

Red followed him in. The interior was

partly in shadow. A quick glance around, however, revealed that there were no horses at all in the building. There were two sets of vertical posts, one down each side, but the stalls had not been completed. In either wall there was a small paneless window for ventilation.

Bart thought he might remark upon the state of the stable to unlock the tongue of the older Harries, who, fairly obviously, had a good deal of authority about the ranch. He half turned, to include Red in his remarks, and as he did so a swinging fist landed upon the side of his head and sent him sideways.

One of his shoulders cannoned off Ike, while Bart was still out of balance. The startled young man recovered himself and drew back from both of them until one of the wooden props encountered his backbone.

'Our father, Abe, is easily taken in,' Ike remarked gravely, 'but we don't let anyone fox us, *amigo*. So we figured that if we knocked a little of the trail dust out of you, you might jest want to tell us what was behind your little game.'

Ike dropped into a crouch, measured Bart with his eye for a punch and feinted, sending his victim closer to the still figure of his brother. Red connected again, high on Bart's chest. The latter parted with his stetson as his head jerked on his shoulders, and at that instant he lost all his apprehension. A tiny flame of anger began to burn inside him. He lashed out in Ike's direction with a boot, and at the same time took a sidelong glance at Red. Ike backed away prudently. Red avoided Bart's first hefty swing, but Ike sustained a sharp blow in the chest when Bart shifted his attack.

The brothers tried to rush him. They scored with a flurry of punches which failed to put him down, and presently, when his breathing was becoming rather laboured, he began to throw fewer punches with greater concentration.

Red developed a swelling under one eye. Ike, now also hatless, collected a bruise on the side of his jaw. Red missed two or three times, but scored rather luckily when a wooden post prevented Bart from getting his head out of the way.

Bart remarked: 'You know, you boys remind me of another fellow I met miles away from here. Name of Harris, Jake Harris, a name not unlike yours.'

Red hesitated and abandoned his latest head-down charge, while Ike lowered his hands to waist level and spoke for the second time.

'Where did you meet him, this Jake Harris?'

For the first time in many minutes all three of them were still. Only the sounds of their breathing filled the stable. Another sound, which told Bart that they had an eavesdropper, came from a window.

'He was in prison, building up his muscles by digging granite,' Bart explained.

His brain was sluggish, but it was clear to him that 'Jake Harris' meant something to these two tough, suspicious, unfriendly brothers.

7

Bart bent over, catching at his breath. He advanced a foot or two, still mindful of where the other two were in relation to himself. He feinted towards Ike and threw a great swing at Red, who this time was too slow to get out of the way. The younger son was clipped on the jaw. He went backwards, tripped over a low stool and landed squarely on his rear with a force which shook the wind out of him.

Bart, still breathing through his mouth a little, advanced in a crouch towards Ike. 'So come on, big brother, you're on your own now. How does it feel to have to act without little brother?'

Ike did not like the way things were developing. Both of the men on their feet knew that Red was not coming back in a hurry. And Bart was smarting over the way the brothers had treated him. His nostrils were flaring and his jaw muscles rather prominent as he determined to get even with Ike.

'All right, Hall, if that really is your name, that'll do for now.'

The voice was that of Abe. The veteran had been listening on the outside to what went on indoors. He had heard the mention of Jake Harris, and now he was in a mood for more talk. Red put a knee under himself, flushed under his father's scrutiny and came to his feet. Ike and Bart took another half-minute to make up their minds. During that time, Bart's arms began to feel heavy. He decided with a shrug that a talk might do more good now. He recovered his stetson, knocked the dust out of it, and advanced towards the door and Abe with a fierce glint in his eyes.

'If this is your doin', Mr Harries, I'm surprised at you. If you have any more dealings with me tonight, I'll come up to the house. But not until I've been under the pump.'

Ike and Red stood uneasily, waiting for their father to say what was to be done. He blinked his eyes a lot, massaged his bristly chin and finally nodded. Bart thought this meant that he was expected. He strolled away, covertly watched by some cowpunchers who had come back from their work. Minus his hat and shirt, he made a good job of washing away the dirt, dust and weariness which he had acquired in the fight, and not until he was feeling much more like himself did he straighten up and give the onlookers a proper view of his features. His face was a bit puffy in places, but he was not badly marked.

The eyes of the men in the bunkhouse showed surprise when the newcomer walked around the house to the front door. He danced up the steps, knocked on the door, and was at once admitted by Mrs Harries, a small thick-set woman with a lined face and a straggle of white hair which had once been red.

She nodded, smiled nervously and handed him a towel. She opened the door into the front room and gestured towards a chair. A couple of minutes later the Harries boys came in from the rear of the house where they had been cleaning up in private. Red's bruised face and Ike's marked jaw looked more noticeable. Abe came in right behind them and indicated where they were to sit, on high chairs. The rancher, himself, squatted on the side of the table.

'What we're goin' to talk about is not business to be discussed in that bunkhouse. Is that understood?'

Abe was pointing a cigar at Bart, who was far from pleased with this line of talk. The young visitor was about to retort in plain language when it occurred to him that Abe had no intention of sending him away from the spread. He said something entirely different.

'I won't go on about havin' your own family beat me up, Mr Harries. So what do we have to discuss that we haven't talked about before?'

'You mentioned a man named Jake Harris. I'd like to know how you came to mention him jest then, and how you came to be in prison.'

This time the questions interested Bart, and he really thought about them. 'I spoke of Jake Harris because something in the way your sons were actin' reminded me of him. Maybe it was the way they went about makin' a fight or something.

'And then again, it might have been the Circle H which Harris had tattooed on the back of his hand. Yer, maybe that was it.'

Three gasps went up from the assembled Harries males. Each and every one of them obviously believed what Bart had said, and they took the tattooing to be a highly serious matter. Once again, however, they acted in a cagey fashion.

Abe came off the table and settled on the edge of an easy chair, padded with a cougar skin. 'How come you were in prison, Hall?'

This abrupt question gave the sons a chance to recover their poise. Bart, however, was in no way put off by it. 'I went there to do a special job. As an investigator I had to get next to a certain character who was believed to know the whereabouts of some old loot. That was all. I encountered Harris quite by accident. I think I know why you're so keen to ask about him.'

The sons maintained their silence, but the old man nodded in an encouraging way. Bart responded. 'I guess Jake is a son of this family. A second son, judgin' by his age. An' he's hit the owlhoot trail, so you don't care to talk about him. Is that so?'

Abe looked up before answering. Bart followed the direction of his eyes. Mrs Harries had stood for a moment in the doorway leading to the back quarters. It was her influence which helped the rancher to come clean.

'All right, so you've stumbled upon the truth. Lots of folks in our circumstances have a boy who's gone wrong. We're no exception. But you'll have to keep this sort of talk to yourself while you're here. And besides, havin' met Jake don't mean we necessarily believe all you told me back there up on north range. So there.

'I'll have to be askin' you to get back to the bunkhouse now, before the hands get too curious about you. An' remember what I said about keepin' a still tongue in there.'

Bart stood up slowly. He eyed all three of them slowly up and down, and hoped that he was mirroring his thoughts. Actually, he was measuring them against his impression of Jake. Moving leisurely, he left the house and made his way back to the humbler quarters of the hired hands.

Although he was not aware of it, two or three men had seen him escorted to the empty stable. They knew what such a visit had meant, and, consequently, Bart was due for a sympathetic reception.

★ ★ ★

The well-heeled riding stranger walked his stocking-foot roan through the buildings of the Circle H a little after noon the next day. Bart Hall was doing a job in the smithy at the time, and he came out into the open long enough to take a brief look at the rider, a man not known to Dick Wood, the blacksmith. Even that brief scrutiny was sufficient to show that this was not Homer Grayson, the journalist, who might have stolen the ring. Bart retreated into his place of work, feeling a trifle disappointed, although he did not know for sure whether this man's arrival had anything to do with his personal affairs.

Wood began to haul another shoe out of the furnace and that was the signal for more striking of the red-hot metal on the anvil by Bart.

In the meantime, the stranger had hitched his horse and mounted the few steps on to the gallery. He moved easily and with an air of self-assurance. Those who noticed him looked him over very thoroughly.

He was just under six feet in height and carried himself with a poker-straight back. His eyes were dark and always in the shadow when his wide-brimmed flat-crowned stetson was in place. He wore a white shirt and a string tie under a neat brown corduroy coat. A single .44 revolver bulged near one hip. The holster was attached to a tooled gun belt.

Mrs Harries was the one to welcome him. She appeared in the doorway of her house, wringing her hands as though she was washing them. The new arrival favoured her with a broad grin.

'Good day to you, ma'am. I've come a long way to be here. Maybe I ought to show you this.' He pulled a ring from a finger of his left hand and offered it to her on his palm. 'There now, you look surprised. But I guess you must have expected to see this again at some time or another. I regret I may be bringin' you bad news. Have you heard anythin' about your husband's brother lately?'

Mrs Harries, who had been given some instruction by her husband, shook her head in an embarrassed fashion and lowered her eyes, having lied.

'Maybe we ought to talk inside. My husband will be back any time. Won't you come in and rest after your journey.'

She glanced briefly into his face and then went ahead of him, into the house. The stranger allowed himself to be shown to an armchair. He removed his hat and sat in the chair, absently replacing the ring on his finger and looking around the room. Mrs Harries escaped to the kitchen, excusing herself in order to make coffee.

There was little conversation between them before the rancher arrived from a visit to the east range half an hour later. The roan hitched to the house rail warned him that something was afoot, and he went indoors with his head down and his brow wrinkled in a frown.

As Abe entered his front room the

stranger, who had been seated in an armchair to one side of the fireplace, came to his feet and advanced towards him with his arm outstretched. Abe showed no warmth, but his wife came into the room from the rear of the house and spoke up.

'Husband, this is Mr Bert Norman from Boston, Massachusetts. He's brought us serious news. It appears your brother has died, an' Mr Norman is carryin' his ring.'

Having delivered herself of this introductory speech, Mrs Harries let out a deep sigh, almost one of relief. She then backed away towards the door by which she had entered. Abe then took a grip of himself. He went through the motions of shaking hands with the fellow who had come to claim part of his estate, but there was no warmth in the greeting.

'Good day to you, Mr Norman. I can't say I'm pleased to see you, seein' as how you bring bad news, but you'd better sit back in that chair an' make yourself comfortable. I reckon you'll be stayin'.'

Norman bent forward slightly from the hips in a sort of stiff bow. He gestured towards the chair which he had occupied before, and when Abe gave no further sign, he dropped into it and toyed with the ring.

Abe tossed his hat in a corner and sat down opposite, producing a pipe and a tobacco pouch. 'How did my brother die, Mr Norman?'

'It was an ordinary case of heart failure, Mr Harries. Perhaps brought on by the rigours of his early life. I don't think he suffered much in the short time between the onset of the attack and his actual death. My mother was greatly upset by his demise, of course, but that was only to be expected.'

In the ensuing conversation, Abe established that this newcomer had been in the state of Nebraska, independently earning his living, when the news of his stepfather's death had reached him.

Shortly after that, Ike and Red arrived home and Abe formally introduced them to Bert Norman, who beamed at them each in turn and thought that they were over-doing the coolness of their response. When the family and their guest were half-way through the beef course of their meal, Abe intimated that Norman had come along with the Harries ring, and that he would be staying.

More than that, the old rancher did not explain, and Norman was sufficiently astute not to make any sweeping demands on so brief an acquaintance. The Harries used the food as an excuse for not saying very much. Abe ate noisily and with gusto. His private thoughts would have intrigued the man who hoped to take over part of the holdings.

Abe was brooding over that letter from Mary Hall, the Boston widow. She had intimated that her son would be along to claim his inheritance. She had even attempted to describe his appearance. At the time when the letter arrived, Abe had been incensed. He had grown so used to getting along without Brad or anyone to do with Brad that the news about a stranger's arrival had not pleased him.

He figured that his own boys had far more title to the estate than anyone horning in with Brad's interests because the two sons had grown up on the territory and worked the land for many years. Now, however, when a seeming impostor was about to cut himself a slice of Harries property, Abe favoured the young fellow named and described in the widow's letter.

He had a notion to let things go along for a few weeks. Maybe this Norman fellow would give himself away as an impostor, or the other one, Bart Hall, would use his wits to show that he was the true beneficiary.

Hall had guts, plenty of sand in his craw, and a useful brain as well. Still looking very preoccupied, Abe finished his meal and walked out on to the back gallery, where he lit his pipe and mulled over his recent thoughts.

* * *

About the same time, Bart was enjoying a game of cards in the bunkhouse, along with Ah Fong, Dick Wood and a happy-go-lucky cowpuncher named Smiler Jones. Bart won more times than he lost. Those who played with him were aware that his hands were not as calloused as some of theirs. This did not seem to put them off him, because at the same time they noticed one or two small cuts on his hands and face which had been acquired in the second stable.

Others before Bart had been along for that special sort of interview with the Harries boys. Bart made no mention of his own clash, and, being Westerners and men who always appreciated a man's right to keep his own affairs to himself, they admired him for his lack of communication on the subject.

The faces of the sons showed that Bart had done quite well for himself in the uneven contest, and the fact that he had not been booted out stood for something else. He was being accepted by the men of the ranch with greater ease than he could have hoped for.

8

During the evening hours the house and the bunkhouse were full of light and apparently good cheer. No one would have guessed that the family were bereaved. Mrs Harries had brought out a bottle of wine, a thing she only did when some important visitor or acquaintance was under her roof. Bert Norman guessed that the wine was not always on the table, and it helped to make him feel that he was accepted by this rather unusual and somewhat conservative family which ramrodded a small cattle empire.

Nothing very much was said about his claims, one way or the other. Around ten o'clock, when the concertina was still playing in the bunkhouse, Mrs Harries showed him into the spare bedroom. A single bed, the longest in the house, occupied almost half of the room, splendidly covered with a bright patchwork quilt.

Norman made a slight fuss over it, and as soon as she had gone he firmly closed the door and began to undress. His ears were alert for conversation about himself, but he was to be disappointed upon that score. Abe exchanged a few brusque words with his sons and the whole family retired without further ado.

The males of the family awoke within half an hour of dawn and started about the serious business of preparing for a long day's work. Mrs Harries, whose Christian name was Selina, shuffled about the house ministering to their needs with a pair of scuffed mocassins on her feet. She knew that there was mischief afoot, and she had no skill in hiding her thoughts from others. All she could do to avoid showing her true feelings to the man named Norman was to stay out of the conversation.

The visitor ate three eggs and a few rashers of ham, starting his meal just as the Harries were finishing theirs. Abe intimated that they would be about the buildings in some place or another, attending to jobs, if he cared to come looking for them. Upwards of a dozen hands spilled out of the bunkhouse within a few more minutes, and one lean cowpuncher aimed a small stone at the rooster which was strutting importantly along the roof.

Norman's innermost thoughts had kept him awake for part of the night, but he was starting this new day of deception with his morale high and with great hopes for the future. In starting this subterfuge, he was aware that he was taking a big risk, but, this far, it looked as though it was going to pay off.

Some twenty minutes later, Norman encountered the owner in the first stable where he was personally attending to one of his favourite riding horses. By that time the hammer was clanking in the smithy and the various everyday work sounds were showing the ranch to be a busy place with an excess of toil for its hands.

Abe straightened up, breathing hard, and took his time in rubbing the horse liniment off his hands. Norman was appreciative of his efforts as a groom and he said as much. Abe slapped the groomed animal on the flank and slowly walked away from it.

Suddenly, he shot a sharp glance at Norman. 'I know you came here with that special ring, and I have no special reason to doubt you at the moment. But you'll understand that me an' my boys have run this ranch for many years an' we don't take to rapid change. I could retire now, but my family don't want it that way. I'm to stay in nominal charge maybe for as long as I live.

'I'm only sayin' this because ours has only been a brief acquaintance. I hope you didn't come along expectin' to take over everything straight away, or a big part of the holdings?'

Norman laughed easily. 'No, I can't say that I did, Mr Harries. I'm satisfied for the moment to have you recognise me for the man nominated by your brother. There don't have to be any rapid developments jest 'cause I've arrived. After all, I know nothin' of the workings of the spread, an' I can't be much of a help until I do.'

Harries nodded heavily, shaking his loose-fitting hat as he did so. He sounded satisfied. 'I'm glad you're that way inclined, Bert. What I had in mind for you this morning was a tour of the home buildings an' a few introductions. Maybe later in the day you could make a visit to town with one of my boys an' make the acquaintance of some of the merchants who supply us.'

'Sounds like a good routine for my first day,' Norman approved.

And with that the tour began.

★ ★ ★

The smith's shop was not a place where the hands were encouraged to hang about during brief rest periods. Consequently, when Norman came around with Abe Harries all that he saw through a heat haze was the scowling face of the blacksmith and the rippling back muscles of his striker. The heat drove the onlookers out in a comparatively short space of time. There was no point of contact between Bart and the latest arrival.

Dick Wood liked to eat his midday meal in the shade behind his work shack. On this occasion, he had persuaded Bart to do the same. They had eaten their food and were contemplating building a couple of smokes when Norman came out of the house and was introduced to a character who had just ridden in from the east range a half-hour earlier.

From the angle of the smithy, Bart watched the introduction with great interest. 'Who's the character with the craggy face, Dick?'

'That there is a fellow called Drag Winster. He's been around the Harries family for rather a long time. A capable, hard-workin' hombre when he puts his mind to it. Used to be a trail boss at one time. These days you might say he was a jack of all trades.'

Wood talked on, but Bart found himself not listening as intently. He was making his own assessment of the character he could see. Drag was around fifty years of age. A man with a leathery face and a bald patch running from his forehead to the back of his crown. His hair otherwise had retained its youthful colour, being dark brown in his jutting brows and his rather tatty down-drooping moustache. He wore a stained check-patterned shirt along with a dark red bandanna. His brown cloth vest was rather shrunken and creased and the brim at the front of his dun-coloured stetson was permanently turned up.

He was slightly above average in height and walked with a noticeable roll as he went towards his mount.

'I would have thought the other fellow interested you more than Drag,' Wood surmised, as Norman and the old cowhand mounted up.

Bart grinned. 'Would you, indeed? Well, I wonder how you figured that out, old-timer? Let's go indoors an' talk some more.'

Moving without haste, they re-entered the building where they worked and presently the conversation turned to other things.

★ ★ ★

An hour later, Abe Harries came and tapped on the window of the smithy, intimating that he wanted Bart out to talk to him at length. Fifteen minutes later, rancher and ex-investigator rode out towards the north, the latter being more than a little curious about this departure from routine.

As soon as they were clear of the buildings, Abe began to open up. 'I don't want you to think that because this fellow Norman has been taken into the house that we are certain he is genuine. In fact I don't think he is. I'm

123

tellin' you this now, an' I hope you'll see that I have a bit of confidence in you.

'I had a letter from your mother in Boston, an' she attempted to describe you. As you seem to fit her description, that goes a long way towards convincing me that you are who you say you are.'

Bart nodded. 'Won't you be runnin' some sort of risk if you keep an impostor in your house?'

'Sure enough, but I thought we might encounter other difficulties if we showed him the door, especially as he has the ring an' a lawyer could do a lot of arguin' on his behalf because of it. So I thought I'd let him stay for a while an' see what developed. Maybe he'll trip himself up, or something.'

'Why have you brought me this far away from the house?' Bart queried bluntly.

'I have my reasons, young fellow. Don't be so impatient. I take it you haven't seen this Norman fellow before he arrived here?'

'No, I never have. And by the way, I told the boys to call me Rider. Joe Rider. That isn't the name I used in prison either, but it will suffice for now.'

Bart wanted to ask more questions, but Abe was frowning thoughtfully and he looked as if he needed time to think. Presently, when they had jogged another four hundred yards further north, the rancher opened up again.

'We talked of Jake Harris the other day. Jake's my second son, as you figured. He was always a difficult, headstrong boy. Ike is my eldest, and as such he takes over from me. Red is different, he can take a back position, but Jake couldn't. He couldn't abide the idea of takin' orders from Ike after my retirement. So he got restless, an' things went to the bad.'

Abe dried up for a moment, as though reluctant to reveal things best forgotten. He was studying Bart's reactions very closely when he resumed.

'I've had it in the back of my mind

that Jake was out of prison. I thought he might have been behind our recent setbacks.'

Bart raised his brows in sudden interest. 'He was certainly still in prison when I left, but I happen to know he did not have much time to do. What sort of setbacks were you speakin' of?'

'Rustlin', young fellow. Our range covers a mighty lot of land. At first it was the east range where we suffered losses, but more recently it's been the north and the northernmost part of home range. Jake is capable of sufficient bitterness to steal from the rest of his family. But I reckon he can't be implicated if he's been put away for some time.'

'It wouldn't be altogether impossible, Mr Harries. I've known men get messages in and out of prison. Maybe he has allies on the outside. Do you think he'd be popular enough with his associates for them to wait for him to be released again?'

Abe nodded vigorously. 'That's one

of the things about Jake. He's a good leader of men. I wouldn't be surprised if one or two of my old hands still have a sneakin' regard for him.'

'If he's out again, an' intent upon robbin' the family, he's likely to show himself in these parts sooner or later. Are you by any chance thinkin' you're likely to lose stock right now?'

Again the older man nodded. 'As a matter of fact I do. The weather and the state of the moon is jest right. We have several hundred head on north range. You probably think I ought to keep a part of my crew up there to look after them, but it ain't all that easy.

'You see, on two occasions I've lost my guard. Once, the fellow was shot dead, an' we didn't find him until long after his death. The other time he was probably shot and his body carried right out of the area. So I can't jest expect any of the boys to take on a night guard job when it's that risky.'

A sudden thought occurred to Bart. 'You ain't by any chance hopin' that I'll take on such an assignment, are you?'

Abe cleared his throat rather noisily. 'I figure you're a little bit green about a cattle range this far. It wouldn't be fair to ask you to take on that sort of a job. All the same, I need protection an' there ain't many men I can call on for this sort of work.'

'I might jest allow myself to be talked into it,' Bart admitted. 'After all, if I'm ever goin' to be accepted at face value by the Harries, I'll have to take a risk or two. So tell me about it.'

Abe gave out with a belly laugh. His thin lined face changed very appreciably as he did so. He leaned back and patted his saddle-bags with a calloused hand. 'I reckoned you might jest be persuaded to have a go, so I brought along a few items of food which I thought you might need.'

This extra show of confidence made Bart join in the laughter. It was several minutes before they sobered up again. This time Bart assumed his characteristic brooding look.

'Now see here, Mr Harries, you wouldn't be usin' this sort of work to get rid of me in a hurry, would you?'

'No, I wouldn't be as cunning as all that. You see, you have an interest in the ranch. You also know my son, the outlaw one. I'm not keen to tell anyone else what I suspect about him and the rustlin' which keeps goin' on. I'm goin' to ask you to try an' find out anything you can by movin' about a bit at night, but I don't want you to take any unnecessary risks. Your background interests me, an' I think you might be able to find out things which an ordinary cowman might find difficult. Anyways, I'm prepared to gamble on you, an' I hope you come to no harm.

'Whatever you do, don't try to take on large numbers on your own. That isn't what I want.'

Bart pushed back his hat and rubbed his sticky forehead. 'You don't by any chance suspect a whole army of rustlers are trimmin' your herds?'

'Not an army, but I think we might

be up against a dozen or more rather than jest two or three. You see, recently they've made off with as many as thirty head. An' movin' at night, that takes a bit of manpower, if you ain't goin' to lose them all over uneven terrain.

'If you want my advice as to where to look, I'd say head due north of the lake, in daylight, an' then work your way westward after nightfall. There's a useful stream of water over on that side of the range known as Brothers' Creek. I have no reason for sayin' so, but I think our disappearin' cattle might go in that direction.

'You see, there has to be a buyer somewhere close, or else a good scarcely frequented route towards the border. I don't know of anyone who would buy them near at hand, so I figure they'll have to be driven some distance.'

Bart massaged his chin with a gauntleted hand. This was skilled work for a good rider with excellent night vision. He thought that in giving him this assignment Abe was paying him a compliment. Brad, the deceased brother, by contrast, had never shown any confidence in him at all. At least, not while Bart was still in Boston.

'If they get their hands on thirty head of good cattle, they won't want to give up without a struggle,' Bart remarked evenly.

Abe leaned across and patted him on the shoulder. 'That's why I don't want you to take any unnecessary risks. Come back and tell me what you find out. I can stand the loss of thirty beeves, so long as the leak is stopped fairly soon.'

Shortly afterwards the two riders moved up the bank of the small lake where they fished for a while, shared a meal and discussed still further Bart's new work as a night hawk.

9

Fully conscious that he was making his first significant effort on behalf of the Circle H, Bart Hall rode away from the area of the lake towards four in the afternoon. Abe had sketched out for him on paper the approximate dimensions of the north range and the vital landmark to westward known as Brothers' Creek. The terrain around the lake was not an area where free-roaming cattle tended to graze, but every succeeding mile further north brought him nearer to the possible hideouts of the rustlers.

He rode, therefore, with increasing caution and a somewhat tiring observation as the sun moved across the sky towards the west. For an hour his direction was due north. After that, he sent the dun through a rich acreage of high breeze-blown bunch grass in a direction approximately north-west.

Brothers' Creek was still far too far away for him to catch a glimpse of it, but he was content to have penetrated so far north without apparently seeing or being seen by any other humans. A few small groups of beeves had gone by. Others were scattered on either hand as he probed about for a hiding place in which to conceal himself until nightfall.

An old buffalo wallow, half hidden by tall grass, loomed up quite suddenly when he was heading for a distant clump of trees. As the dun slithered down into the depression he made up his mind to stay in the hollow while he waited for the sun to sink.

He dismounted in the very centre of it, wondering if there was water close under the surface. A brief inspection of the soil suggested that he might dig for quite a while and find nothing, but there was no real necessity to dig for fresh water. He had a canteen containing water only, and another which held water laced with whisky. Abe Harries had been thorough in his preparations for the night vigil.

The dun was glad to be rid of the saddle. As soon as it had got over its restlessness, he poured some of his precious water into his hat and offered it to the thirsty animal in true cowpuncher fashion. After that, there was plenty of time for a thorough grooming with handfuls of grass and a short-haired brush.

Pressing thirst finally drove Bart to see to his own needs and he drank some of the water left in the first of the canteens. Ultra caution made him decide against lighting a fire on which to cook a meal, but he did roll a few cigarettes and he thought that the tobacco had never tasted better.

His food consisted of a few biscuits and pre-fried bacon mixed with a small tin of beans. Out in the open he liked the smell of a wood fire, and he promised himself that if he survived this night's possible clashes that he would camp out in the future for the sheer joy of doing so.

He had been lying on his back on a soft slope for half an hour when the sleepiness of the open-air life put him into a light doze. He stayed that way for longer than he would have thought, and when he roused himself and heard again the bawling of the beeves on all sides the sun was well over to westward and the night shadows were beginning to roll across the land.

He saw to his equipment then and took out the spyglass for the first time. The depression had served him well as a place of concealment, but now that he wanted to be able to see things at some little distance round about, he began to see that it had its disadvantages. Unless he raised his head well above the grass, he could not see for more than a few yards.

In the middle of his first careful observations, he gazed longingly at the clump of trees not more than a furlong distant. Clearly, he had to stay where he was now until the light had gone, but he could not help wondering how things might have been if he had missed the hollow in his ride and gone straight through to the timber stand.

After making two slow circuits of the saucer, he gave up trying. He was tiring himself unnecessarily, and the amount of his observation this far was not worth the effort. If he was lucky, his ears would serve him a whole lot better than his eyes in the event of unwanted activity by trespassing renegades.

Soon he was relaxing again and seeking to train his ears to pick out the sounds of mouthing, hooved animals from the other noises of nature.

Darkness, which fell fairly swiftly, left him blinking for a while. Dusk brought with it its own peculiar form of loneliness. Bart found himself visualising without effort the interior of the rough but comfortable bunkhouse at the Circle H. He could image the superficial, but pleasing, humour of men who spent most of their lives as nurses to beasts on the hoof.

He sighed a few times and brooded over the problems of running such a big outfit as the Harries ranch. Two men had died on this same chore as he was contemplating now, that of night guard to scattered groups of bawling long-horns. Now that the testing time was coming, he wished that he had spent a whole lot more hours listening to the protesting cries of these self-same animals, so that he could perhaps detect special noises put out when they were afraid of something unusual.

His imagination played him up for a time. He began to see things through the moving, sighing grass along the upper edges of the hollow. To improve matters he had to take his attention off things visual for a time and turn his thoughts inwards. He stayed like that for a while and only changed his attitude when a group of steers which had settled to the east of him started to bawl all over again.

He crept to that side of his hideout with his heart thumping. He had out his Winchester now, and it was likely that he would be tested in accurate night shooting if what he suspected turned out to be rustlers in large numbers. He stared, waited and listened. After a disturbed ten minutes the cattle noises started to fade again, as if they were more contented, as if some unknown disturbing factor had now been removed.

Bart moved his position a yard this way and a yard the other. There was nothing at all to engage his eye from the east. During his moves he noted that a bleak moon was now scudding through cloud and that the whole range had taken on a faint glow. This was the sort of condition which Abe had mentioned earlier; what he thought was an ideal rustlers' moon.

The stars prickled the canopy of the heavens and helped to distract the tense young man in the hollow. And then the first of several small noises put him further on edge. He heard something which sounded like a hoof striking hard rock. Not the unshod hoof of a cow, however, but the metal shoe of a horse. He thought he had seen a spark fly up some little distance towards the northwest, but having had the impression for a while, reason made him think that he had seen it only in his imagination.

Three or four minutes later he had a similar experience. This time he thought he detected the hoarse cry of a mounted rider with a dry throat. There was activity now among the cattle to the north and also in other groups further west.

A dawning intuition made him almost sure that he was not alone any more. He felt that there were men, although they were not particularly close. He decided upon a sortie on foot. This brought a snicker of protest from the dun, but he managed to calm it with a few choice words and soon he had scrambled out of the wallow with his spyglass and his weapons, hoping to make closer contact with the intruders he felt sure were about.

Distance, in the dark, played tricks upon him. He walked in a wide circle, stumbling every now and then over a hole or a thick clump of grass. He had almost circled his starting point when a faint flicker of light at a much greater distance than he would have expected finally confirmed that there was some sort of rustling operation in progress.

He judged the direction to be between north and north-west, and the flash of light which he had seen, possibly the uncovering of a lamp, had occurred at anything from a furlong to double that distance, or possibly more. Lack of experience of this sort made the estimation of distance practically impossible.

He surmised that if cattle were driven, they would move towards the west and the watercourse known as Brothers' Creek, and they would go fairly quickly when the drive was started. Consequently, he darted back to the wallow, almost fell down to the lowest depth of it in his hurry, and started to prepare the dun for a speedy departure.

In the dark he made a good job of rigging the blanket and the saddle, but it occurred to him that it would have been better had he done this before the light faded. Some five minutes later he had checked over everything, and he coaxed the willing animal up the short steep slope to the level of the terrain above.

★　★　★

The activity to the north-west had the effect of making other groups of cattle bawl. In the first hundred yards or so, Bart was distracted from the actual terrain ahead and the way in which the horse was coping in the dark. He found himself gazing first in one direction and then in another.

The sounds of the beasts made him wonder if, in fact, Abe Harries had far more cows up in this part of the spread than he had intimated.

His mind was still full of conjecture

when the dun stumbled in a small hole and involuntarily stopped. He saw then that he was putting an undue strain upon it. Without its help he could be in a very vulnerable position if the rustlers detected him. At once he slipped to the ground and proceeded again on foot. He led the quadruped and was pleased that it did not need a lot of coaxing.

Some five minutes later, with a breeze blowing towards him, he stopped walking and wondered what his best plan of action was to be. A few choice rifle shots might have the effect of startling the rustlers and spoil their plan, if they really had one; but such a course of action would also have a signal effect upon the various groups of sleeping and resting cattle. He had heard about stampedes and the way in which they could decimate a herd. The numbers involved here could not be so described, but if they panicked and scattered in all directions the ranch might lose more beasts than if the rustlers had misappropriated them.

He shrugged unseen in the night and plodded forward again. The breeze in his direction would help to conceal his presence for a while longer, but in a very short time he was almost bound to be in contact. After that he could expect violence. Would he be victim number three?

Very shortly after that the two dusty focal points of noise up ahead of him converged. Next, he heard voices. The rustlers were acting in a much bolder fashion, shouting at the beeves like ordinary drovers would. Through a thin haze of dust which rendered the darkness almost opaque he saw the light of a swinging lamp, further left than he would have expected.

A high-pitched hoarse voice, which apparently went with the lamp, gave advice to the clandestine drovers. It was indistinct to Bart, but he managed to get the gist of it.

'Keep below me, boys, otherwise you won't hit the bridge! You hear me? You're gettin' close right now!'

Bart paused again. He was gripping his reins as if they were his lifeline. As he pondered once again what to do, a startled white-faced steer came blundering out of the darkness and headed straight for him, swerving aside at the last second to miss horse and man. Bart wondered if he was directly in the path of one of the moving groups, but his anxiety on that point soon faded. The beast he had encountered was only a stray.

Coughing gently on dust, he mounted up again, and draped the blue bandanna which he had adopted for ranch work across the lower part of his face. A droll thought occurred to him as he did so. He was wearing the mask of the road agent, whereas the rustlers of the range no doubt left their renegade features bare for all to see.

Two or three strays barged across his path in different directions. It was the drumming of unshod hooves on wooden planking which told him that the creek was near. This far, its placid sounds had been drowned by the other activity.

He turned the dun and headed more directly towards the bridge. The ghostly light of the lantern came and went as the beasts passed in front of the guide. Through a positive sea of dust, he followed in the wake of the longhorns and the men who were stealing them.

The light went out quite abruptly. The thunder of hooves on wood continued and grew louder as the dun covered the last hundred yards to the bridge. Suddenly the hoof sounds were muted as they struck earth on the other side.

Bart was as wide awake as ever as he glanced round in the dusty atmosphere, looking for a drag rider, a man looking after stragglers at the tail of the group. He did not see one, and this surprised him. Men's hoarse cries came from the other side of the stream. They sounded confident, as though they had already achieved what they set out to do.

The bridge had recovered its silence

145

for perhaps three minutes when the dun first set its fore hooves on timber. Bart allowed it to proceed. He had the feeling that he was acting after the event. Some night hawk he was turning out to be. And yet what else could he have done, other than a wasteful firing off of weapons?

His thoughts were still on the subject of firearms when he approached the half-way mark. The bridge was a crude, strong erection paved with thick wooden ties, and supported in the middle of the water by a series of wooden piles, driven in in a line.

At either extremity, a low wooden rail about two feet above the ties prevented beasts and horses from blundering over the edge into the creek water. When the muzzles of the three rifles started to belch flame from the other bank, the dun sidestepped towards the rail on the south side.

The marksmen were spaced out over about ten yards. Their aim was along the bridge itself. The ineffective night hawk had been observed before the crossing. Bullets were threatening to cut him down at any second when he called for a big effort on the dun's behalf.

Whinnying with fear, it leapt the rail on the south side with its hide still intact and dropped precipitately towards the water. At the same time, Bart kicked his feet clear and lunged to one side. He entered the cool waters and was rendered hatless before he had proper time to straighten out in the air.

He, too, this far appeared to be unscathed.

10

Down Bart went, trailing bubbles and still shocked by this sudden change in his fortunes. Abe had been right when he counselled extreme caution. As soon as Bart had made a move to take him into contact, he had run into trouble. They had known that he was on that bridge and that he was not of their company.

He tensed his throat muscles and made sure that he did not breathe while under the water. Moss brushed his face. Altogether, he could only have plunged downwards for a second or two, but it seemed longer. His hands were free and he used one of them to rip the bandanna away from his mouth. That gave him a slight feeling of satisfaction, and then his forehead was brushing the bottom, which had a goodly covering of tree branches and twigs, all broken off the creek-side trees at an earlier date and since lodged there.

He checked his forward progress and tried to think constructively. Air was his next consideration. That and the avoidance of flying bullets. Fortunately, he knew sufficient of his surroundings to be able to swim towards the east bank. He did this and cautiously broke surface after swimming some twelve yards in the right direction.

Even after that short time his boots were beginning to feel heavy. Riding boots were about the worst possible kind of footwear for swimming under water. Fear prickled the back of his neck as he gently stroked for the unoccupied shore and awaited a further flurry of lethal bullets.

None came straight away. He swam on, eased his aching chest and filled it again. Diving from the surface he submerged to a depth of about six feet and continued to make progress on a powerful breaststroke.

It was not until he was underneath

again that he had the time to think about what he had learned during his brief respite. Men were shouting on the bank where the danger lay. At least one of them was running up the bridge. He, evidently, was seeking a vantage point for the kill — if it had not been already achieved.

Downstream a few yards there had been a turmoil. He knew, now that he had the will to assimilate the information, that the dun had caused the disturbance. Something about the way it had hit the water had given it more cause for fear. In its early struggles it had lost its balance and rolled in the water.

Later, Bart was to reason correctly that this commotion in the water had won him a useful breathing space. The majority of ordinary cowpunchers were not at home swimming in deep water. Usually, when there was an accident they tended to hang on to their mounts. The rustlers had expected this, and in searching for the man around the horse they had failed to locate him.

About a minute later an encroaching underwater root came into contact with his arm. He grabbed it, held on and cautiously broke surface right above it. Only an inch or so of his head showed; enough for him to breath and to peer back towards the bridge and the other bank.

The man on the centre of the bridge was panning his rifle this way and that, willing the victim to show himself but being anything but keen to fire at ripples. On the other bank, two men, whose spurs were jingling quietly, moved apart on the slope, using storm lanterns to help in their search. They were checking on the west bank to see if a man was swimming ashore or floating that way.

Carefully watching the bridge gunman, Bart slowly surfaced on his back. He edged around the protruding roots and contrived to work his way further inshore, into a tiny inlet. An object three feet away gave him a fright, but it was only his hat floating upright on the surface.

'Ain't no sign of him along this bank, boys, but there goes his cayuse! Hey, you there on the bridge! Randy! Get yourself over to the other side and give the horse a lookin' over!'

'You want I should bring the cayuse back with me, Lofty?'

'Nope, we got all the horses we need. Jest make sure that hombre didn't slip out of the water holdin' on to the horse's tail, or anythin' clever like that. Then get yourself back here as soon as you can! We done got rid of the snooper by the looks of things, but Harries might have other tricks up his sleeve we don't know about!'

Bart surmised that the dun had scrambled out about fifty yards further down on the same side as himself. The man addressed as Randy hastily went on his errand. He appeared to go as far as the spot where the dun had emerged. Bart wondered if he was exploring the saddle pockets, but other small sounds made by the horse led him to think that the rustler had merely contented himself with looking around for the rider.

Randy paused within twenty yards of Bart's hiding place, causing a certain amount of alarm, but the swimmer's luck held. He remained unobserved while the searcher answered a brief call of nature. Long before Randy had rejoined the others, Bart's attention had shifted to the main group.

Three or four men were now conversing in rather loud tones as though they had the whole world to themselves. What they had to say was very revealing, even to a man with some water in his ears.

'How come we didn't get word from the ranch about Abe sendin' a night hawk up this way, Lofty?'

'Aw, don't let it bother you. Our boy at the Circle H can't cover every little happening. You can rest assured his information about the next event will be up to date and reliable.'

'What sort of an event are you talkin'

about, Lofty? I thought we were all in the know on this caper!'

The last speaker had a deep voice. He sounded disgruntled. Before Lofty answered he let out a peal of laughter. 'You got a surprise comin', buster, you an' the others, all. I can tell you now that Jake's back! We shall all meet him tomorrow. He's at the usual spot west of here, an' what's more he's plannin' something big to grab for himself a sizeable chunk of the family fortune!'

'Jake Harris is out of jail an' back here on his home territory?'

The deep voice sounded barely convinced, but another took over the questioning, and Bart found himself standing up in the muddy shallows with his streaming head well clear of the surface. Purely due to luck, his reconnaissance was beginning to pay off. The enemies of the Harries were actually shouting valuable information at the tops of their voices.

'Are you hintin' that Jake is about to snatch bigger bunches than we've taken in the past? Is he that mad with his family?'

'He's goin' to hit them so hard before the end of this month that Abe Harries will be glad to hang up his boots an' sit in a chair for the rest of his days!'

The precipitate return of Randy broke up the exchanges for a minute or more, but he quickly convinced the others that the swimmer had not left the water on the other side. Randy then started to ask his own questions.

'How are things goin' to be for us in the future, Lofty? Will Jake look after us? After all, we've waited for him for a long time. We could do with some rewards, couldn't we?'

A whole chorus of excited voices drowned any early response, but eventually they quietened, and the voice of Lofty reasserted itself.

'I reckon Jake has always known how to look after his own kind, but don't go gettin' greedy, that's all. If he takes on any partners it ain't likely he'll promote us. And if he brings in any new faces, don't go grumblin' about them. He's been about quite a while since he saw us last, an' he'll maybe be a bit edgy after that spell in jail.'

Something spooked a few head of cattle at that juncture, and it served as the signal to start the rustlers on their way again. Bart wondered if he ought to try and tag along behind them to find out more, but his recent experiences made him decide otherwise. Besides, there was much that Abe ought to know, as soon as possible.

Five minutes after the intruders had left the far bank, the temporary night hawk set about drying himself out, prior to a speedy return.

* * *

Dick Wood, taking a short ride on a horse he had just freshly shoed, was surprised to encounter Bart in the first of the timber behind the Circle H home buildings. He responded at once when Bart demanded to have the boss come out without delay and parley with him.

So it was that by half-past eight in the morning Rancher Harries was being brought up to date. Anger, excitement, indignation and intense frustration showed in his face before the deep hurt occasioned by the knowledge that his second son was back in the area and prepared to rob him wholesale.

'You reckon he's goin' to hit us before the end of the month? On a large scale? Well, don't that make you think.' Something in the back of Abe's eyes made Bart think that he had an idea how the spread might suffer, but for the present he did not reveal it. 'We've got a renegade right here in our midst, boy. Up until now, you done real well an' my boys would join me in sayin' as much, but I wonder if you think you've done enough? Are you hankerin' to get back in the smithy, or to learn a few tricks with a brandin' iron?'

Bart draped an arm over his saddle, resting his weight on the dun. 'I figure if I survive there'll be time for that sort of thing. Right now you need to know who it is who gives out information. Before this crisis happens to you. Bein' an investigator I could help some more. But where do I start?'

Abe started to walk about in small circles. He was worried. He knew every old hand and yet he could not mention anything which would give Bart a lead in his search.

'It has to be somebody who comes an' goes fairly often,' Bart prompted.

Sudden thought registered behind the older man's eyes, but he still refrained from making helpful suggestions. 'You have a free hand. Tell me anything you want an' I'll have Dick bring it out here for you. That way, you don't get involved with small chores an' you can watch an' follow anybody you want.'

Abe handed over a useful amount of folding money, and a half-hour later the blacksmith returned, as promised, with everything that a man could need to keep him in circulation for a few days. Bart thanked Dick, asked about how

Norman was settling in, and finally sent the curious tradesman back to his everyday chores.

★　★　★

At two in the afternoon, Bart was lightly sleeping in a grassy hollow about fifty yards back from the private Circle H track which led towards Bonanza Springs. Working alone, he had decided that he could not watch the comings and goings on all sides of the ranch. He had chosen to keep his watch on the town side.

Five minutes after two the unmistakable sounds of a mouth harp coming from the direction of the ranch shook him out of his afternoon lethargy and put him on the alert again. He had cleaned and oiled his weapons after the dowsing in the creek, and now he was ready for new emergencies.

The musician on horseback was Drag Winster. His playing of the mouth harp on lone rides had a disarming quality about it. Bart wondered whether a visit to town behind Drag might be profitable or not. A vision of Abe's face, baffled as it had been earlier, during the revelations, made him stop trying to reason things out. All the old hands had to be suspect while the search was on.

Five minutes later, Bart hit the trail in the wake of the craggy-faced individual. He kept well back and hoped that he would have no difficulty in nosing him out in town.

*   *   *

Drag Winster must have increased his pace in the last mile. He had vanished from view himself, and he had been thorough enough not to leave his horse pawing the ground by any obvious hitch rail. Bart viewed his disappearance with mixed feelings. Drag might have something very private on his mind, but there was nothing to show that he was working against his boss. Nevertheless, he was in town, and he did have more freedom than most of the ordinary hands.

Bart searched for upwards of half an hour. He avoided the office of the town marshal as he did not very much want it to be known that they had talked earlier. Three saloons and two eating houses showed no signs of the missing man, and by four in the afternoon the young investigator felt for the first time like making the best of a bad job.

There was a man who sat habitually outside a certain saloon, and this was a person Dick Wood had said he ought to cultivate. Bart stood in the shadow of a sidewalk awning and regarded the character in question who was occupying a bench on the other side.

Link Claybourne was his name. He was over sixty and he had not worked for the Harries for several years. Nevertheless, he had done enough in his working days to finish with a good reputation, and men old and new who still drew Harries money continued to offer him liquid sustenance.

Claybourne was a gaunt individual whose frame was shrinking in his old trail clothes. In recent months he had taken to wearing a black blanket poncho over his shirt and vest. This made his appearance more distinctive. Bart wondered if he had the habit of selling information to his former employer's enemies. But this scarcely seemed possible. On the other hand, if Claybourne had a free tongue he might be in a position to help. Putting on an ingenuous smile, Bart crossed over to him, offered his hand to be shaken and lifted the empty beer glass which stood on the bench.

'The name's Joe Rider. I'm a new employee at the Circle H. Hang on a minute while I get you some more beer.'

The arrival of the beer took three minutes, but Claybourne did not seem to mind. 'Take the weight offen your legs, Joe. Sit a while. I see most of the Harries boys some time or another. I don't reckon you're a local man. What brought you to these parts?'

Men came and went on the side-walks, but none seemed particularly interested in the drinking conversation-alists. Bart thought quickly. He decided to spill a little information in the hope of getting some back.

'I'm a native of the east coast, but the west has always drawn me. I was workin' in Kansas when something happened to send me this way. I met a man in Boston, an' when he died recently, something happened to make me think I had a good future with the Harries family.'

Claybourne nodded and blinked. He grabbed his glass with a talon-like hand and drank about a third of the contents. Bart watched his Adam's apple working and then was distracted. Thirty yards up the sidewalk a man had stepped out of a shop and started to come towards them.

The man in question had on a different coloured hat from the one remembered, but his pockmarked skin and dark, restless eyes were the same, and he was dressed similarly in a dark suit, a white shirt and a black cummerbund. Bart had thought him in Fort Worth, but here he was, in the flesh. Recognition was sudden in Grayson's eyes. He lowered them, turned on his heel, tugged at one of his big flat ear lobes and started to go through the motions of lighting a cigar.

Having recognised him, Bart did not want him to slip away before they had exchanged words, but a deep feeling of bitterness prompted the young investigator to use an approach which was normally foreign to him. He raised his voice and continued the conversation.

'I met a man upstate from here, a fellow who claimed to be a journalist in Fort Worth. I liked him when we were together, but after he left me I was robbed, in Woodford. The things which were taken were vital to my future, an' only this newspaper man could have known anything about them.

'So he must have been implicated in the robbery! I ain't seen him since, but right now that there fellow lightin' that cigar is his spittin' image! An' he's one man I need to talk to more than most! Hey, you there! Homer Grayson, if that's your name. Come along this way an' talk to an old friend! If you walk away now I'll know you're guilty!'

The man thus addressed was seen to stiffen. He was Grayson, all right, and he knew that he could not avoid a clash with the man who was calling him. His back straightened, he pulled on his cigar, moved it in an airy gesture wide of his body, and then he started to turn with remarkable speed.

Bart was on his feet in a flash. He sensed rather than saw the revolver in Grayson's right hand, and that was the warning to take instant evasive action. He let go of his beer and dived sideways away from the bench and the man sitting on it. His dive took him off the sidewalk on to the street. A bullet chipped the boards at Claybourne's feet. Another kicked up a furrow of dust a foot away from Bart.

As his hat rolled away, the young man executed a sketchy cartwheel and came on to his feet again, his .45 in his fist. A third bullet hit dust between his feet, and then he was firing in return. His first lifted Grayson's hat and the second, aimed slightly lower, ripped into the journalist's chest, just to the left of the sternum.

Grayson at once twisted, lost his balance and fell to the boards, dying. Bart moved to him slowly. Grayson lifted his gun an inch or so, but his failing powers made it go down with a clatter. His eyes closed as Bart came above him.

Holstering his gun, the younger man looked for signs of life. There were none. As Claybourne advanced to look over the dead man, Bart recovered his hat and waited for developments. Ten to fifteen sightseers slowly encroached upon the area. One of them purloined the cigar.

Marshal Lobo Farnes came through them on silent feet. He removed Bart's gun from its holster and looked on over his shoulder, breathing through his mouth and seemingly troubled by this sudden development on such a warm, quiet, uneventful afternoon.

Link cleared his throat. 'I witnessed everything, Marshal, from start to finish. The dead man drew first an' without warnin'. It's my belief he had a bad conscience over something that happened earlier between him and this young man from the Circle H. Hadn't we better go along to your office an' talk?'

'If you think that's for the best,' Farnes replied quietly.

He sent one of the onlookers to locate the undertaker and the doctor and, presently, in his office, he received a few more pointers to the way in which the brief lethal clash had gone.

From the creaking chair behind his desk he surveyed his two visitors. 'Tell me, is that dead man anything to do with that robbery you mentioned at our earlier meetin'?'

Bart scratched his chin and glanced sideways at Claybourne, who raised his eyes innocently and offered no comment.

'You can safely talk in front of Link, mister. Most folks do that, but he can be discreet when it's called for.'

'Okay. The dead man is the one I thought might have turned up as the impostor, but I was wrong there. He represented himself to me as Homer Grayson, a newspaper reporter from Fort Worth. He was the only person who knew enough, I thought, to stage the robbery in Woodford. I'd say there has to be a connection between the impostor, who has arrived, and the dead man. Impostor's name, so he says, is Bert Norman. He's jest beginnin' to find his way around.'

Farnes whistled quietly. He blew along the length of his moustache before asking further questions. 'Does Abe trust you after what's happened?'

'Sure, he's learnin' to do that. I'm supposed to be an ordinary cowhand called Joe Rider at the moment. I'm tryin' to find out who might be leakin' information to a powerful gang of rustlers from across Brothers' Creek.'

Claybourne cleared his throat and shrugged under his poncho. 'You might jest be interested to know that Drag Winster and another fellow turned up on the scene right after the shootin'. Other fellow had on a cord coat. He had an eagle's beak nose and bristlin' sideburns — brown in colour. They took a close look, made sure the other fellow was dead an' then lit out fairly fast. They'd remember your face if they saw it again.'

Bart let out his breath in a long sigh. Clearly, he was thinking hard and he appeared to be making some progress.

'Would this stranger be the impostor you talked about?' Farnes asked.

'That's him, all right, Marshal. Bert Norman. I'm real glad I met Link, here, now. Maybe the two of you could keep quiet the real reason for my bein' in the area? I'd like it that way, till the opposition tips its hand.'

Farnes rose to his feet and strolled to the window, inserting his thumbs in his waist belt. 'Okay, okay, we can do that much for you. You don't need to trouble your head any more about the shootin'. An' tell Abe that if he wants my help at any time, I ain't wholly in the dark. Take your gun, an' reload.'

'I'll do that,' Bart promised as he led Link out of the office and went in search of more beer.

11

Bart hoped for a glimpse of Winster and Norman together, but he was disappointed. They had gone to earth with the same efficiency as Drag had shown earlier in the day. To show his interest and gratitude to Claybourne, the young investigator stayed with him for an hour, and after that he wandered again.

Quite by chance he encountered Marshal Farnes on his rounds. The peace officer was strolling with the town's doctor, a stiff-built sixty-year-old with a short white moustache and clip-on spectacles. Dr Gibbons carried his hold-all in one hand and nervously brushed down his dark suit from time to time, as though he was fearful of germs acquired on his rounds.

Lobo was happy to see Bart again, because the medical man was a great talker and meticulous in his methods. Form fillers embarrassed him.

'You really ought to have that signed statement from the man who fired the gun, Marshal,' Gibbons was saying. 'It's the only way to carry out your job. Besides, somebody might come along and ask for details of what happened, maybe after you've left office.'

Lobo made the introduction, and Bart, having overheard a little of the conversation, intimated that he had been on his way to find the marshal with a view to signing his statement. Hearing this, the doctor relaxed in his attitude and begged to be excused. Farnes sighed with relief. Back in his office they drew up the statement. In it, Bart intimated that Grayson was a thief who had robbed him, and no mention was made of Harries' affairs.

As Bart was about to leave again, Lobo offered him a bit of advice. 'If you're still lookin' for Drag an' his friend, try Widow Bates' place on Second Street. That end. It's jest a possibility you might want to try.'

Bart thanked him for the suggestion and withdrew. By that time Link Claybourne had withdrawn from his usual pitch for an early evening siesta. An hour had gone by when Bart's vigilance was rewarded. He saw from a distance of a hundred yards that the two men in whom he was interested had emerged from the rooming house and were in the act of mounting up.

Their horses were to hand in a small enclosure behind the building and their saddles were in place. It appeared that they were about to leave town. The chances were that they would head back to the ranch, but the observer could not be certain. He wished then that he was still in touch with Claybourne, but the old man might have been anywhere.

Only one course lay open to the investigator. He had to recover his own horse. He found it where he had left it, in a small corral at the back of a livery stable, and after giving it a hasty rub down, he cinched up and swung into the saddle.

As he passed the office, which fronted on to the street, he parted with money to cover the time he had left the horse, and then he was on his way, moving at a fast clip up the street of dirt and wondering if once again he was likely to lose his quarry.

About four hundred yards out of town the Harries private track began. The prints of the two riders showed in it and confirmed that they were ahead. Some of Bart's enthusiasm waned at this stage, but he recovered it again a good mile further on when the shoe prints turned off the track and struck a new route further to the south.

Now his mind was full of speculation. So far as he knew the Harries had no near neighbours on that side of their territory. Nor could he think of any reason why a newcomer seeking a future in management and ownership should be interested in that side of the Circle H boundaries.

Bart turned off where they had done and increased his pace a little so as to catch up with them, or at least bring them within surveillance distance. Ahead of him the ground undulated so that in a comparatively short time he caught glimpses of them as they negotiated high ground.

Clearly, their destination was well ahead of them. They were not likely to go to earth much before nightfall. If he was to learn anything from this protracted ride he would have to school himself to be patient. This he attempted to do without delay.

★　★　★

Up ahead of him the two riders were not in a very happy frame of mind. Drag had been using a lot of tact since they left town. In doing so he was a little bit out of character. Norman kept moving his lower jaw in a chewing motion, although he had nothing in his mouth other than his tongue and teeth.

175

'I keep tellin' you, Drag, it ain't any use you bawlin' me out. Not on a day like this. It ain't every day a man comes up the street of a strange town an' finds his own brother jest gunned to death. I don't like it. Right now we ought to be somewhere back there, closer to town, an' layin' an ambush for the fellow who did it! That's more what I'm used to, an' I figure Jake would see it my way, too.'

Drag clicked his tongue. 'I can guess how you must feel, but don't try an' solve all your problems yourself. Hear me? You're under an obligation to Jake. It's best to talk to him first, especially as he's plannin' something real big in the near future. You got to lick your wounds a while. Things will turn for the better real soon. You'll see.

'Back there in town it wasn't the right thing for us to show ourselves. So think ahead to Jake, an' see what he'll do to restore your family honour.'

By way of an answer, Norman halted his stockingfoot and refused to go on.

Winster, who was annoyed, kept a poker expression on his face and acted upon impulse. He backtracked about fifty yards, checked his mount under a tree with low branches and climbed up into it.

This move took some of the determination out of Norman, who watched him with growing curiosity. Some three minutes later, Drag started on the descent. Norman called quietly to him, but Winster would not answer until he was ready. He dropped into his saddle, gripped his horse's barrel and soon put himself alongside of his riding partner.

'That jasper is right along behind us. He's left the Circle H track, an' that proves that he's deliberately followin' us. He must have been lookin' for us when he ran into your brother this afternoon.'

'So why don't we jest hang back an' ambush him from these trees?' Norman asked. 'Ain't nobody to see what happens to him, an' we'll be doin' Jake a favour.'

Winster slowly shook his head. 'You and I know Jake differently. Let him do the executin', if that's what he wants. Maybe he'll want to question this hombre before anything happens to him. After all, it would be interestin' to hear what he has to say about that killin' an' him followin' us out here. After all, he never did get to see us when your brother was killed!'

'All right, if you're sure. So let's push on. We don't want him to get within gunshot distance in case he's out for more scalps. But I sure do hope Jake understands about how I feel on the day of my brother's death.'

Drag made the right sort of noises. He said things and he clicked his tongue sympathetically. At the same time, in his private thoughts he was reasoning that the two brothers, Grayson and Norman, as they were known, were not necessarily the best types to work for a man like Jake Harris, who had a quick temper and a swift way of eliminating unco-operative underlings.

Grayson had already paid for his piece of initiative in Bonanza and Norman might just go the same way if he tried protesting too strongly with the Harries' second son.

★ ★ ★

Bart was surprised when he heard the playing of the mouth harp. Somehow he had not expected it on this trip. The use of it seemed to suggest that Winster was completely at ease, and that was probably a good thing. It meant the old cowpuncher had no idea that he was being followed and, consequently, Bart could relax.

He did so, as far as the other riders were concerned. The ride took him across a part of Circle H east range, and through a shallow stream where horse and man were able to refresh themselves. It was pleasant for a man who liked that kind of travel. Inevitably, however, as the last hours of daylight went by with the sun dipping towards the west, the time dragged. Bart marvelled at the things which had happened to him since he last slept in a bunk.

He had been shot at, thoroughly soaked in escaping from a bridge ambush, and then subjected to a street shoot-out. Now, he was on the prowl again, seeking to find out things about renegades who preferred darkness to daytime. He began to feel slightly chilled, although there was still plenty of warmth in the air.

East range slipped behind, and a fairly stony barren stretch followed across the southern extremities of ranch land. Rabbits and a wildcat were the only moving things which Bart noticed, other than the birds.

In the last hour of daylight, the route of the leading pair changed again. They headed towards the northwest and the sounds of running water. Their silhouettes were becoming difficult to pick out as they crossed wide, shallow water on horses reduced to a walk. On the far bank they loomed higher for a few yards and then disappeared.

Bart followed after them, through the shallows and up an earth bank beyond which had been pushed up there by man. He should have been warned at that stage, but for once his senses let him down. Perhaps it was because of the fairly steep drop down into the natural basin on the other side of the mound.

The dun snickered in surprise and promptly squatted back so as to retain its balance on the way down. Bart hung on with his legs braced. The shoed hooves dug deep sandy grooves in the soft soil. The lower branches of encroaching trees sought to brush the rider out of the saddle and then they were at the bottom. The group which most interested the young investigator was round a slight bend to the right, where a low Apache-style fire had been lit.

There he saw seven or eight men, all dressed in trail garb and taking their ease, although their attention was on him, and a mere suggestion of hostility on his part would have started something difficult to finish.

A tall man in their midst was holding a pancake or something of the sort over the top of the fire. There was something in his stance that hinted at his identity, although he kept his face averted.

'All right, amigo, that's far enough!'

The voice surprised Bart when nothing else should have done. It was that of Bert Norman, the impostor. Norman was to one side, his body resting against a tree. Keeping his hands still, Bart peered around in the other direction. There, he saw the chunky face of Drag Winster. Drag had another long-barrelled revolver lined up on him, and on this occasion Winster's face showed more antagonism than that of Norman.

'This is the fellow, Jake! Followed us all the way from Bonanza,' Winster explained. 'I reckon we've got him right where we want him an' no questions need be asked!'

There was a murmuring from the men around the fire which seemed to suggest a lot of sympathy for Winster's point of view. Norman's voice was slightly off-key when he joined in.

'An' what's more, he shot my brother to death this afternoon right there in the middle of Bonanza! He ought to be seen off in cold blood!'

Bart knew that he was really up against it now. Only a colossal bluff and a great deal of luck could see him through this crisis. Now, he had to play upon his brief earlier meeting with Harris in prison. Although his heart was secretly thumping really hard, he put on a bold face.

His laughter baffled the two men who had their guns trained on him. He pointed towards the fire. The bold grey eyes of Jake, almost hidden under the brim of a big Texas hat, were watching him closely. With his free hand Harris mopped his bony forehead and the long line of his lantern jaw, dabbing at his face with the edge of a gaudy red bandanna. He removed the flap-jack from his wooden fork and turned to face the developing situation.

'If that there ain't my old buddy, Jake Harris! Doggone it, you sure do make it hard for a man to find you once you get clear of prison, amigo!'

Deliberately ignoring the threatening guns, Bart swung to the ground and started across the sandy earth in the direction of the outlaw leader. Harris allowed him to approach, although one of his hands was free and in a position to dip for a gun, if that proved necessary.

Other men drew their weapons and one or two hammers clicked before Bart was in hand-shaking distance of his one-time fellow jailbird.

'You followed me here?' Harris queried in a low voice.

'Not exactly, Jake. I came ahead of you. You haven't forgotten I know about the tattoo mark on the back of your hand?'

Harris pushed the last of the flap-jack

into his face and munched it. His jaws were still busy when he brought up his left hand and examined the device on the back of it by the glowing light of the fire.

'Are you tellin' me you escaped from jail an' came all this way, to Bonanza, in Texas, lookin' for the Circle H? That's a lot to believe, some might say, Arthur!'

They continued to stand toe to toe and Harris' last question had sounded ominous. 'You have a Texas accent, Jake. I don't figure there's another Circle H ranch in the whole of this state. So here I am!'

Harris swallowed the last of his food, and this time he laughed, but his laughter ended abruptly. He was still trying to take his unexpected visitor by surprise.

'You been to the ranch, my father's place!'

'Of course! Where else would I look than at the family ranch? I was surprised not to find you there, an' I began to think you might never show up. But I had it somewhere in the back of my mind that you would soon be back this way. So I kept watch, an' this afternoon, not very long after I'd dealt with that jasper in town, I noticed these two fellows, Winster and Norman, ridin' an unexpected trail. Imagine my surprise when they led me right to you an' your boys, out here in the middle of nowhere!'

'All right, all right, so you've come an' I suppose you want to join the outfit. There's jest one thing we might have to settle between us before we offer you food. Norman is sick about his brother's death. What am I to say to him?'

Bart pretended to be puzzled. He raised his voice a little so that it would easily carry to the nearest of the rustlers.

'The man Grayson drew first. I beat him to the kill an' that's all there was to it. If Norman wants satisfaction tonight, of course I'm prepared to give it to him. It would be a pity, though, if two brothers had to die on the same day, within a few hours and a few miles of each other.'

Norman and Winster, along with most of the others, had by this time reholstered their hand guns. Without turning round, Bart added a few choice words in a lower tone.

'Of course I won't keep on sayin' that he was a side-windin' son of a thief an' that he deserved it.'

Harris nodded and patted him heavily on the shoulder. He strode away from the fire in the direction of the other two who had recently arrived.

'Norman, I don't think you have grounds for quarrellin' with this man who followed you in. I'd forget about it, if I were you, mainly because Arthur, or whatever he calls himself these days, is an old buddy of mine. He did me a few favours while I was in prison.'

This latter revelation took the wind out of Norman, and Drag Winster's face became the background for a series of rapidly shifting emotional scenes. The tension had lifted in the rustlers' camp, at least for a time.

12

BART slept well in a place close to the fire between Jake Harris and a man named Lofty Valance. Valance had a closely-trimmed down-drooping moustache and rather off-putting protruding eyes. His high-pitched hoarse voice sounded familiar and Bart felt sure that he had done a lot of the talking after the shooting across Brothers' Creek.

In the hour after dawn, Bart awakened a few minutes before his associates, but he feigned sleep for a while longer in order to get his thoughts in order for what was likely to be a testing and critical day.

As soon as the coffee was bubbling and the men were moving about the young investigator stayed close to Jake and talked about prison life. At first, Harris glowered, but soon he was rejoicing in the knowledge that his old enemy, Brownwood, was still 'inside'.

There was plenty of bacon for breakfast, but the meal was taken in haste. Harris himself ate as swiftly as anyone and it became clear to Bart that he was supposed to eat quickly, too. Evidently, Jake had done quite a bit of thinking during the night and there were to be exchanges between the two of them before the day was much older.

'I'd like you to stick around here, by the fire, for a few minutes, Bart, while I give a few instructions.'

Bart signified that he was prepared to take the advice. He slowed down on his rate of eating and casually observed what took place. One after another, the men left the area of the fire and moved down the draw, going out of sight around a towering outcrop. Somewhere beyond that natural obstacle there were cows. Perhaps just a handful, or possibly more. Their numbers at this stage did not interest Bart greatly. He was more intrigued to know where they were going. Any question along these lines, however, this early in the day was bound to promote mistrust.

While he was engaged in kicking sparks out of dying embers, Jake returned. The outlaw leader had with him his own horse, a big roan with a white blaze, and Bart's dun. He intimated that they were going for a ride, almost immediately. Jake mounted up first and started back over the ground which Bart had covered on the way there.

As soon as they were across the shallows the talk began. 'I thought we might ride this way. Sooner or later you'll want to go back that way and show yourself. You won't mind if for the present I keep one or two secrets to myself?'

Bart nodded and grinned. 'What sort of talk did you want to make, Jake?'

'You'll know by now I'm not on terms with my kin. Do you happen to know how my father reacts to rustlin'?'

Bart shrugged and dabbed his neck with his blue bandanna. 'He reacts in

190

an angry fashion, Jake. No man likes losin' cattle to thieves. I hear him talkin' sometimes, an' what he has to say makes very interestin' listenin', you can be sure.'

'What other talk does Pa have in mind?'

'Well, there's this hombre who calls himself Norman. I don't know how well you know the fellow, but he claims in some way to have title to part of the Harries land and cattle. Would you be surprised to know that Abe has Norman figured for an impostor?'

Jake whistled and Bart was impressed with his surprise. Hall wondered if he was being too frank, caught as he was between the two camps. Any study of his own position, however brief, brought the younger man out in light perspiration. For the first time in his life he had an insight into the doings of two hostile groups. More than that, he was involved with both, and at this particular juncture either side might be forgiven for trying to blast him apart.

Playing the part of an investigator was one thing. Being a spy, however unwilling, was something else; something totally undesirable. And yet, in a way, his destiny had to some extent been mapped out for him. The arrival of the ring after Brad Harries' death had been the biggest surprise of his life. Very little of what had followed had been planned.

'My old man must have sharp faculties these days. Tell me, how did he know Norman was an impostor?'

'It seems he had some mail. From Boston, up the east coast. Written by a woman who had married your uncle, Brad Harries. In the letter she described her son, the one who was to be the beneficiary. The description didn't fit Norman at all. Right now he's in a funny position.'

Jake slowed his mount and reached into his breast pocket for his tobacco sack. He was adept at rolling smokes when other men's nerves would have spoiled the effort. Bart watched him with a mounting fascination. Jake tore a paper out of a small book, rolled it between his fingers and started to spill tobacco into it.

He succeeded, licked the edge of the paper with his tongue and completed the making. Bart accepted it from him and put a match to it while Jake went through the same process again. The brand of tobacco was a fragrant one and Bart derived some pleasure from it, in spite of his rather difficult position.

Jake drew on the second one, which was rolled slightly thinner. 'An' the strangest thing of all is that Norman thinks he's fully accepted. Can't say I like Norman all that much. He's more of a confidence trickster than a cattle operator or bank heister. What do you make of him?'

'It's difficult to have special feelings about him,' Bart replied, rolling his smoke to the corner of his mouth. 'I guess he's doin' what he considers to be his special job in life, conning some-body for money.

'Rest assured, Abe will get rid of him, if he stays very long. Abe's good and angry, too, about losin' thirty or so head of cattle quite recently. He's bound to tumble to your whereabouts an' your presence quite soon, Jake, an' he'll hit you an' your outfit with quite a large number of guns. Maybe you will push him too far. I wouldn't rely on the fact that you have blood ties to keep you out of serious trouble if he decides to use his men on a large scale as gun slingers.'

'Ah, to hell with Pa!' Jake remarked, colouring with anger. 'He's unfortunate, in a way. I should have been born the eldest son, an' then he wouldn't have all this trouble over what's goin' to happen when he's dead. Besides, I'm a good cattleman, even if I have to steal my stock.

'I've decided to do something about my share of the estate. Thanks for your warning, but I think we shall have made our strike before Pa gets really militant. Later this month he's startin' quite a big herd on a cattle drive to the north. I aim to hit that herd when it's one day's march clear of Circle H range.

'I intend to take it over, every last animal, an' run it to another place where I'm settin' up on my own. You have to hand it to me, that's the way to operate! Hit somebody hard an' in a big way! That's the way *I* operate, Bart, an' if you want in on my scheme you only have to say so. I can see I've shaken you a little bit by my revelations.'

Bart was mildly stunned when his mind registered how the rustlers were going to hit the trail drive and take over the cattle. In order to do so, they had to be prepared for a wholesale shoot-out, and at a time when one or other of Jake's brothers might be involved with the riders. He was trying to think out how the ambush would be carried through when Jake broke in upon his thoughts again.

'You ain't said, yet, amigo. Are you figurin' on joinin' me, or do you have other ideas?'

Bart grinned. 'I came a long way to join you,' he lied, 'and after you've offered me so much of your confidence I could hardly back out now.'

'That's the way I was figurin' things. But I wouldn't have said so much if I hadn't been sure of you. Right now, seein' you have a job at the ranch you'd better be gettin' back there. Keep your ear to the ground an' if anything unusual develops, don't hesitate to pass the information to Norman or Winster. They'll get it back to me an' I'll act on it. How about the trail drive? Were you figurin' on goin' along with the drovers?'

'You're askin' too far ahead, Jake. I couldn't rightly say. Tell me, do you fully trust Norman an' Winster? It seems to me a confidence trickster might try to outsmart his buddies as well as his enemies.'

Jake massaged his jaw with a gloved hand. 'I don't figure they'll doublecross me while this big deal is cookin'. On the other hand, it wouldn't make me sad if they didn't stay with us long.

Winster I've known longer than Norman, but he's grown awful close to Norman in a very short time, an' that ain't always a healthy sign.'

Both horses had been halted. They were now milling around one another while their riders took their farewell.

'What would you do if your brothers happened to be among the drovers when your boys struck, Jake?'

Harris hesitated for a mere second or two. 'A man with my outlook on life can't afford any sentiment. When I go off anyone, I go off them for good.'

'You don't need to say any more, Jake. *Adios*, an' remember, I'll have your interests in mind.'

Harris raised his right hand briefly in salute, turned his horse and began his return ride. Bart, for his part, rode towards the Circle H track wondering if he was likely to survive the coming clashes and whether his self-respect would ever be the same.

13

THE following eight days, those prior to the eve of departure for the trail herd, were trying ones for the men involved in the known and the secret preparations. Bart Hall was in no way at ease. He believed that the family still had confidence in him, but there were times when one or other of the Harries boys came near him and he felt that he was under some sort of special surveillance.

Twice the young investigator engaged in private talk with his boss, and twice more he was in touch with the enemy. One clandestine meeting took place between himself and Norman at the back of the cookhouse late at night, and the other was a brief encounter with Winster on the way back from the east range.

On that day the hands were very busy. No less than five hundred head of cattle were brought from the east range and other sources ready for the protracted drive north next day. By late afternoon most of the preliminary herding was done and the cowpunchers who were not still polishing their saddlery or weapons were sitting outside the bunkhouse yarning and drinking coffee.

Abe Harries came out on his front gallery looking preoccupied. He raised his hand, obviously wanting to contact somebody, and Winster was the first to acknowledge him.

'I'd like to talk to Rider over here, please.'

Bart, who had been leaning against the wall exchanging stories with Smiler Jones, heard his name called and detached himself from the others. Once or twice he had been asked whether he was going with the drovers or not, and he had been forced to say that he did not know the boss's mind. Now, at this late hour, he was obviously going to get some kind of instructions. He hoped that the Harries men were not going to panic at this late hour.

'It's about that search for water on the Lazy T property, Joe. I'd like you to ride over to the Blean place tomorrow, or you could go tonight if you feel like gettin' off to an early start.'

Bart put some show of reluctance into his step as he approached the gallery. 'I suppose it's necessary for me to do this chore, Mr Harries. I mean, wouldn't I be of more use on the trail drive?'

Abe chuckled to himself. 'You're learnin' fast, laddie, but there's still things you have to be taught. No, I want you to stay back here with me while the drive is on. I'm sendin' both my boys, also Bert Norman, so you'll have plenty to do while they're away. Now, about this source of water. If you care to step inside, I'll show you a rough map so you'll find the obvious spot more quickly. Come on in.'

Abe had the map laid out on his front-room table. He showed it rather briefly, and indicated where the water was likely to be found on the nearest neighbour's spread to the north-east.

'I'm sendin' you away now, Bart, because I want you to have a free hand. Also on this table is a map which shows the ground where the herd is likely to rest on the first night out. I'd give more time to that, if I were you. Try an' get help from Jim Blean. He won't like what you have to tell him because he's plannin' his first small drive a week or so after we leave. But he might co-operate. See what you can do. The boys an' me, not to mention their mother, want to tell you that we all have confidence in you.

'If at any time your future depends upon a showdown with Jake, don't hesitate to take any sort of action to keep yourself alive. I don't like havin' to say this, but I think my brother's choice was a good one. We think you'd be more good in the long run around here than our boy, Jake, even if he had a complete change of heart.'

Having made his little speech, rendered in all sincerity, Abe glanced around at the others for their approval. All three showed it, particularly was it obvious in his wife. Keeping clear of the window, Bart shook hands with them all.

'I'll do whatever I can over at the Blean place. If they don't agree to help you boys, count on meetin' up with me the first night out. The very least I can do is spring a few surprises.'

Ike, seeming slightly out of character as he tried to make conversation and be friendly, showed Bart to the door. 'Mind you don't lose that map, an' don't fail to give our best wishes to the Bleans. Tell them we hope they don't have any special problems on their first drive north.'

'I'll do that, Ike, an' please tell your father I'll be settin' out for their place before nightfall. I'm curious to have a look at that sandy area where the spring might be. *Adios*.'

Ike nodded curtly and withdrew. Bart

went back among the boys, talking of this and that. Most of them felt sorry for him because they knew he wanted to go on the drive and they thought he was bitterly disappointed. Fifteen minutes later, having filled his saddle pockets with various easily-carried eatables, he took his leave of the excited ranch hands and rode off towards the north.

★   ★   ★

That night Bart camped out alongside of the lake where he had first met Abe Harries. The area was entirely deserted and he was in no sort of a hurry to get to sleep. He spent two hours and more going back over all the happenings since the time when he had met Jake Harris in prison. The overall time involved in this remarkable sequence of events was relatively short, but a great deal had been packed into it.

Now that he was so thoroughly involved with the Harries family and the big showdown was so close, he was able to wonder quite calmly if he was likely to figure in the reckoning after the clash with the outlaws, or whether he would merely be mourned over a short period as an unlucky contender.

If he had the misfortune to be struck down and killed by a bullet, there was little doubt that his remains would find an open-air grave somewhere along this strip of Texas territory so well used by the owners of the longhorns. Such an end, however, had little to commend it.

Long after he had finished his food, in a sober frame of mind he wrote down his thoughts about coming events upon a scribbling pad which he had acquired at the ranch. Even though his diary was not to hand, he still liked to unclutter his mind a little at night by writing down his thoughts.

He curled up his long body in two blankets as a chill breeze blew along the surface of the water. The last thing he remembered doing was glancing up at the remote dark sky and willing himself to come awake at dawn.

Jim Blean, a limping ex-miner and ex-prospector who had been coerced into becoming a small-time rancher by an ambitious wife, waved to Bart from the rail of his front veranda a little after eight o'clock the following morning.

'Howdy, you must be Joe Rider. My boy, Zack, brought a message back from old Abe last week. We were expectin' you, an' you're welcome. You came about our search for water, of course, but Abe hinted that there might be something else of a very serious nature to discuss. Did he say anythin' about that?'

Bart stepped up on to the veranda and shook hands, while Jim called into the house for his son and his wife to join them.

Jim was a poker-faced fellow, about the average in height and lean of frame. He had a peculiar tuft of greying brown hair on the end of his chin which gave him some sort of distinction. His only son, Zack, was a dark, moody-looking youth of twenty with hunched shoulders. His small head looked bigger because of the tall undented dun stetson clamped down upon it.

Mrs Moll Blean was three inches taller than her husband, a determined-looking bony Irish woman with high cheekbones and a look in her eye which brooked no nonsense from men, whether they were her kin or simply hired hands.

Bart shook hands with these two in turn, murmuring his pleasure at the greeting. While he was busy, men sauntered out of the bunkhouse which stood back a bit from the house and wandered across to find out what was going on. In front of them was a freckled, blue-eyed, capable-looking Irishman with a knowing look on his face.

For a few seconds Jim Blean looked a little bit put out by the other's approach, but, feeling his wife's eye upon him, he made an effort to appear both jovial and helpful. 'This here gent approachin' at the head of my boys is my foreman, Paddy Mahearn. He's mighty keen on findin' the water, 'though it doesn't interest him quite so much as the whisky he likes to drink in town.

'Meet Joe Rider from the Circle H, Paddy. And the rest of you boys. Joe has been sent along here with information about where to find water. And there's something else he has in mind, too. So squat down some place an' listen to what he has to say.'

Bart shook hands with Paddy, who seemed to be more interested in Mrs Blean than her husband. He wondered about the possibility of a marital problem, but he soon pushed his thoughts to the back of his mind and unrolled the first map. In doing so the second one fell to the ground, where Mahearn picked it up with a modest show of curiosity.

Now that he had to talk, the visitor was keyed up. 'It was good of you to give me the chance to talk to everyone together, Mr Blean. The fact is, the

Circle H is desperately up against it. We have sure factual knowledge that a big gang of outlaws is plannin' to snatch the whole herd durin' the night one day's march away from home.

'If you could see your way to helpin' us, Mr Harries would be eternally grateful to you. He's plannin' to take almost all his fit hands into the reckonin' to fight back, an' that means that the herd will be unattended for a while. That's where you could help us.

'We wouldn't want you to get too involved, seein' as you have to run your own herd in a few days. But we would appreciate the kind of help I've mentioned. May I ask what you think about it?'

Bart went quiet. First of all he scanned the faces of the hired hands to note their reactions. He found them varied and interesting. A couple looked profoundly shocked. Others were beginning to redden with excitement. Paddy Mahearn looked as if he was sizing up the possibilities of making a name for himself and seeing a bit of action at the same time.

'I don't know that I could ask my hands to take part in what you have in mind, Joe, even though we're in sympathy with any troubles you might have. After all, we're hopin' to run our first herd north next week, as you know. Comin' right before our own big effort it don't seem fair to ask my men to help.'

Jim's eyes seemed to be sliding away to the face of his son, as if perhaps he did not want the boy involved in a fast trading of lead at his tender age. Mrs Blean moved restlessly about one end of the veranda. Bart noted this, and it occurred to him that Mrs Harries also exercised a good deal of influence in her own quiet way.

Paddy Mahearn had picked out the mistress's restlessness. 'I think we should help, if only as drovers for a time. After all, if the Circle H boys manage to kill off or drive away this gang of rustlers they'll be doin' us a favour. For don't we have to cover the same territory next week?'

Four or five youngish cowpunchers spoke up in support of the foreman, who had the knack of swaying people to his way of thinking. The owner, who was still troubled about who would go and who would not, sensed the general atmosphere and asked a question.

'Do I take it that you, yourself, Paddy, would ride out with some of the boys an' help our neighbours?'

'You do indeed, Boss. I'd ride out with *all* our hands to help the neighbours. It would be good trainin' for boys who haven't struck trouble on a beef trail before. You'll give your permission?'

All eyes turned to the figures on the veranda. Jim's hesitation was scarcely perceptible. 'I give permission for all to go who want to, barrin' perhaps young Zack here, who ought to get in a lot of sleep before he goes away with our own cattle drive.'

Zack looked as though he was going to protest, but his belated chance to give his opinion was drowned in a noisy chorus of approval from the enthusing ranch hands.

Bart thanked them all. He took coffee and more food to fill his saddle bags, and led Paddy Mahearn and ten more men away from the Lazy T that same afternoon. They made a brief stop at the spot where Abe had said water might be located, and then they were pushing their mounts hard in order to get far to the north of the two ranches well ahead in time of the drovers and the herd, not to mention that other determined team of men who were planning to molest them.

14

ALL the way north, with Jim Blean's boys hooting and whistling in carefree fashion, the coming clash seemed totally unreal to Bart. As he rode, his mind ranged this way and that, and sometimes he had to handle the map which Abe had sketched out for him to make himself believe it was all true.

In mid-afternoon, when the riders had grown quiet due to the oppressiveness of the sun, Paddy Mahearn had a few questions to ask, and that helped Bart to think out the details of what he was going to do with the volunteers.

Bart answered him and added: 'I know I'm pushin' everything a bit hard, Paddy, but a great deal depends upon you an' your boys gettin' into position before the rustlers place themselves out. They'll be along early, because they have this big action planned, and because they can expect the trail crew to be tired on the first day out. That means startin' to bed down for the night early.'

Mahearn held up his hand. 'I know how you must feel about what's going to happen, Joe, an' I won't question you any further. Jest call out for a rest when we get level with that gully you mentioned. Given fifteen minutes off, the lads will be glad to walk their mounts into position. After that, they can relax.'

'I'll do that, Paddy, an' I'll be glad of the break myself.'

Bart went back to his map reading. He would have liked to feel relaxed, too, but he knew that was expecting too much. Instead, he unconsciously increased his pace.

* * *

On the first day of a long haul, a travelling herd was as restless as any member of the human team in charge of it. Most droving crews pushed the animals hard at the outset in order to work the bad temper out of them and to settle them down to the routine of travelling several miles a day.

Ike and Red Harries were quite orthodox in the way they handled their herds, and this particular day was no different from any other starting day. Most of the time the brothers rode ahead, at the important positions of point. That meant that they scouted the ground ahead of the herd, one a little to each side of its main route, and kept a look-out for obstacles: gullies, waterways and anything which could cause chaos among their obstinate bovine charges.

They took it in turns to ride further ahead than was customary and, where the terrain permitted it, they spent a short while together talking about the menace which lay ahead of them. At two in the afternoon they had one of these spells.

'Brother, we've got to put the word

around the boys that something is afoot. It'll be too late when they're bedded down to start the explanations.'

The speaker was Red. They were still discussing what was to be done when Bert Norman started to come forward from the flank of the herd with the intention of joining them. Ike was the one who came up with the idea.

'When he gets up with us, we keep him here, out of the way. Make him work point opposite you. I'll drop back on some pretext or another an' I'll work my way round the whole team. How will that do?'

Red nodded in agreement, and a few minutes later the plan was put into being.

The Harries brothers knew the lie of the land better than anyone else. Ike had finished his chore connected with the warning of the riders, and his horse was on the tired side when the last mile or so before the expected camping ground began to go past underfoot.

Drag Winster, back in charge of the

chuck wagon after a couple of spells at home, was well ahead of the others. Red could see when Ike rejoined him and Bert Norman up ahead that there was something troubling him. Drag was used to acting on his own initiative. It was just possible that he might go a little further than the site which the Harries had anticipated for the night camp. If he did, his action might cause difficulties for the Blean riders and others.

'Everything all right, Ike?' Norman asked as the three riders came together.

'More or less,' Ike returned with a forced smile. 'We're gettin' towards good campin' land, however, an' there's plans I'd like to make. Red, I'd like you to ride forward so as to stop Drag missin' out on the early sites.'

Norman started to make an offer, one which Ike had anticipated. The impostor was waved into silence. 'I know you wouldn't mind takin' off after that rascal on the chuck wagon, Bert, but I'd prefer it if you'd part company with us for a short while and make a survey of that strip of water on the west side. Think you could do that? It might not last long so close, an' we don't want to make things difficult for us the first night out.'

After a few seconds' hesitation, both Red and Norman agreed to Ike's suggestions. When they had ridden off, the eldest son gave out with a heart-felt sigh. He started to mop himself down with a damp bandanna. At this stage, all those who were to be relied upon had been told to expect action later on. He wondered what they were all thinking, especially as he had warned them not to discuss the matter with Norman or Winster.

Over a slight rise, the first groups of longhorns started down towards the thick meadow-like triangular patch of grass which Abe had sketched out for them. Ike began to relax a little more when he saw that Winster and the chuck wagon had been overtaken and that the chuck wrestler was already running the horses out of the shafts a few yards to the right of a shallow depression where they had planned to have the fire and put down the bedrolls.

Drag waved to Ike and the latter waved back to him, indicating that he was satisfied with the site chosen. Shortly after that, Bert Norman started to come back from the west and the waterway, using for the operation a dry gorge which would prove ideal for a night attack by sneaking gunmen.

Ike waved to him as well, but he could not help shuddering as he thought how different things were likely to be after dark. If Jake Harris had laid his plans as thoroughly as they were led to believe, then Norman must have already seen signs of them.

Ike rose in the saddle. He pointed out the meadow grass up north of the camping site and the dry gully. Several 'punchers acknowledged him and the bunched groups of the herd started to walk and run on to the chosen patch, already seemingly aware that they were due for a long rest.

Ike exchanged shouted information with Norman, who was very confident that they had chosen well. 'The water is jest deep enough for them not to want to cross over when they've drunk their fill, Ike,' Norman informed him.

'I guess that's so, Bert. Maybe now you'd like to have a powwow with Drag, seein' as how you ain't talked with him since first thing this mornin'. Better watch out, though, 'cause he always has plenty of chores to do for unsuspectin' fellows.'

Norman acted upon the suggestion, cutting through the advancing beeves and trying not to show his impatience to be within conversing distance of the cook. Gradually, the beasts began to settle. Five minutes elapsed before the first of them were tempted down to the water's edge, and by that time Ike and Red were sitting their horses in the shallows to make sure there was no build up of barging or milling cattle as others scented the water and came down the slope.

Most of the tired cowpunchers hung back, watching from a distance and reasonably confident that the brothers had the whole herd in check. Seemingly of their own accord, the mounts of the two brothers gradually moved closer together.

Red spat confidently into the stream. 'Can you see anything interestin', brother? Anythin' we ain't supposed to see this early?'

Ike looked around in all directions, taking great pains to make sure that they were not overheard. 'I ain't seen nothin' of the rustlers who ought to be somewhere over this side of the herd. On the other hand, that jasper Bert Norman had a very shrewd look in his eye when he left the stream and rode up that gully.'

Red nodded and bent low over his horse's neck. 'Seems kind of uncanny to think that brother Jake could be real close an' plannin' to blast us all to hell later tonight. If the Lazy T boys an' Joe

Rider are in position, they must be on the north side of this meadow, down behind that barrier of low shrubs. Think they'll be there?'

'There's a lot of reasons why they might not be, but I'd gamble they're around an' I'm not usually a gamblin' man. The herd seems to have learned not to push over takin' on the water, so let's quit this spot and see how the camping arrangements are developin'.'

Red nodded. They emerged about fifty yards apart and made for the hollow on the near side of the wagon. As they did so a few bars of mouth harp music filtered across to them as Drag limbered up for a couple of lively numbers. They went forward slowly, shaking their heads over him.

★   ★   ★

A half-hour later all the hands except Smiler Jones, who had clicked for early evening guard duty, were round the fire smoking and relaxing over coffee and taking in the savoury smells of Drag Winster's roasting beef.

The old hands were convinced that Drag was not in the same high cooking class as Ah Fong and arguments developed. One or two men were of the opinion that he probably tried hard on the first night out and most of them agreed with that because he was most active in his preparations and they were all griped with hunger.

Another half-hour went by before the roast was ready. Ike and Red were suspicious about the food, as they had been over the beverage, but apparently nothing had been tampered with. They were to be allowed to eat and drink well, whatever had been planned for them afterwards. Winster acted as though his cooking was some sort of a test. He talked about it and watched closely as the men ate it. If his conscience was playing him up he covered it well.

Two fellows who had been riding the flanks undertook to clean up the plates and other utensils and this freed the chuck wrestler for further entertainment on the mouth harp. He played consistently and well for upwards of two hours, during which time the men smoked and sang and drank and told noisy jokes about experiences on other drives.

All this time, Ike and Red were nervous. Ike was glad of his reputation for being taciturn. He could think of little to say in the circumstances. And Red was scarcely more at ease. The action started to happen as far as the trail herders were concerned when Drag stopped playing, gave out an enormous yawn and pointed to the wagon where his night roll was.

The sun was dipping and the whole landscape was slowly filling with shadows, minute by minute. Bert Norman was one of the men who stood up when others turned their attention to their rolls.

'It's me for the first two hours of darkness as night hawk,' he explained.

'An' anyone who tries to argue against that is a fool.'

No fool took him up on that. He mounted up on his stockingfoot roan, gave them all a wave and headed for the perimeter of the big meadow where the cows had settled. For nearly a minute he waited with his head held high, and then he decided to circle the herd anti-clockwise. Norman was superstitious, and he hoped that he had made the right choice of direction for his critical piece of work.

Only a pressing excitement kept the Circle H hands from going off into a deep sleep. Further north, beyond the bedded beeves, Jim Blean's outfit was just as restless. They had seen the arrival of the trail herd, and that had excited them. For quite a time they had watched for interlopers on the waterside, but the rustlers had moved with such skill that they had shown no signs at all of their presence.

Paddy Mahearn and Bart Hall watched as the roan plodded past them less than fifty yards away. It was only with an effort that the foreman managed to withhold his questions until Norman was out of earshot.

'Is that fellow on the roan loyal to Harries or not?'

'He's an impostor, hopin' to horn in on Harries property. I don't doubt that he has something special in mind, in takin' on as first night hawk. Keep your eye on him, Paddy, an' don't let your boys make any noise.'

'Are you pullin' out?'

'I'm goin' over there to the camp to eliminate the other traitor. Let this fellow keep on with his job, if nothing develops quickly. I'll come back an' deal with him myself. Probably he'll be busy for two hours.'

The two men shook hands and parted. Bart made a sizeable detour, walking his dun around the rear of the chuck wagon and making his approach with extreme caution. So successful was he that no one around the fire had heard anything before he stuck his head out of the tailgate and called to them.

'Boys, this is Joe Rider talkin'. Drag Winster is now secured an' he won't utter a peep until the action is over. The attack might come any time, probably up that gully from the water. If it doesn't develop soon, wait till the fire flames go down a bit and then creep out of there. Go towards the bank of the stream, keepin' south of the gully. An' good luck. I'm hopin' to take care of Norman myself.'

Red murmured: 'We're with you, Joe. Don't take any chances. Seems to us the area round the creek is quieter than it ought to be.'

Bart acknowledged. He then dropped out of the wagon on the other side and started to work his way back to the east side of the herd.

15

As Norman circled, and the flames of the fire died down, Jake Harris raised his arm at the creek end of the dry gully. In response to his summons fourteen men moved slowly and quietly to join him. All their attention was focused either up the gully towards the fire-glow and the shadowy outline of the wagon behind it or to the north where the cattle were grouped.

Somehow all their heads came reasonably close to his. He looked them over and nodded. 'Boys, you made the quietest crossin' of all time. I was proud of you. No man made any unnecessary splashin', an' that went for the horses as well.'

He glanced briefly behind him to a narrow spit of sandy soil, a sand bank, in fact, which stood out from the bank and yet was hidden by hanging foliage.

No less than fifteen riding horses were patiently standing on that narrow strand. They might have been trained in a school for rustlers' mounts.

Lofty Valance tapped Jake on the shoulder and pointed assuredly in a certain direction. 'That'll be Norman,' Jake explained, 'actin' as night hawk for the first two-hour spell. If he wants us to attack in a hurry, he'll get in touch. Otherwise we'll proceed up this gully, and the main consideration once again is silence. Everybody understand?'

There was an excited outburst of whispering, which Jake allowed to go on for a while so as to take some of the tension out of his men. By the time it was dying down he found himself beating a finger tattoo on the stock of his rifle.

'When we go, we go easily. No racin' to be there first. Any questions before we proceed?'

'How can we be sure that Drag Winster ain't in our line of fire when the shootin' starts?'

The speaker was stocky, bow-legged Randy Pleese, who had failed to locate Bart Hall on an earlier occasion.

'Drag has his orders to keep away from the fire. I guess he'll stay right there in the wagon till the fun starts. Him bein' cautious when the chips are down. Rest assured, he won't be anywhere near your bullets when you open up, Randy. Don't let any consideration like that put you off.'

Jake gestured for his men to spread out. This they did at once, and a couple of minutes later they were crawling slowly and quietly up the gully to the scene of action.

* * *

As Bart approached the eastern perimeter of the big meadow, alive with hundreds of resting beasts, his nerves took a beating. It started when a tiny chain on the dun's harness began to affect him with its muted jingling. He found himself believing that any listening man within a large radius would be able to hear it.

Presently, as he stood in the darkness half-way between the fire area and the meadow, his obsession with the chain made him abandon his horse. He found for it a small cropping place between six or seven sizeable boulders and hoped that it would stay there. As he took his requirements from the saddle and prepared to depart, it tossed its head and stared after him. Fortunately, it did not make any significant noise, and so the general calm continued to prevail for a while longer.

So keen was Bart's mind that he imagined the approach of Bert Norman at least three times before the night hawk actually appeared upon his circuit. On the back of the stockingfoot, the full silhouetted figure in the corduroy coat was slumped already through his long day of unaccustomed horse riding and the encroaching coolness of the night air away from the fire.

When finally Bart was sure that

Norman was approaching, he sank down to soil level and made his preparations for the ambush. He could still hear a faint movement towards the south-west as one of the last of the retiring ranch hands trailed the leather surface of his chaps through a patch of thorn.

Harries' men had made their retreat in fine fashion, and now Bart was alone in the immediate area, except for Winster who was trussed, and the outlaws under Jake Harris, who might be close or still at the far end of the gully.

Bart watched the mounted guard approach. He was riding still in the same direction and now coming away from the north side of the gully to circle just wide of the fire and the wagon. Flickering firelight illuminated the guard for a few seconds and then he was past the spot, and no sort of movement on his part had revealed whether in fact he was still alert or asleep.

Bart rose into a standing position not more than ten feet in front of the stockingfoot. He had his Winchester up to his shoulder before the plodding animal could give the alarm, and when Norman looked up the muzzle of the shoulder weapon was aimed directly at his trunk.

'That's far enough, Norman.'

Norman checked the horse with his knees. He raised his hands slowly above his head and blinked hard, using his eyes and wondering what new move was afoot. Presently he identified the still, threatening figure ahead of him and he gave out a quiet exclamation of surprise.

'*Rider*? Is that you? You ain't supposed to be here. Abe said for you to stay back at the ranch. What's goin' on? Why the gun? Is this some sort of a hold-up? Who are you actin' for?'

Norman put a lot of feeling into his voice without being foolish enough to raise it.

'Let's have your weapons, impostor.

The rifle first an' then the belt and the guns at your waist. Do it very carefully because my nerves are a little on edge. You don't want to act the way your brother did. The disease he died of might be catchin'.'

Norman snorted angrily. He lowered his rifle most of the way and then dropped it. Presently, and not before he had considered playing some sort of a trick with it, his gun belt followed. It dropped heavily, weighted with the pair of twin guns which he wore habitually. Neither of them went off, and although Norman tossed them in such a way that Bart could not see them without straining, the young investigator was satisfied that Norman had carried out his orders.

'Now what do we do?' Norman asked in a thoughtful sounding voice.

He was thinking that Joe Rider was a cool customer, if he had turned against his old prison acquaintance, Jake Harris. Such a switch took a lot of nerve on a night like this. Norman still thought he was the smarter of the two. He did not have to wait for the crawling rustlers, even if they were close.

'You turn that cayuse around, keep it still an' then dismount on the usual side. Start movin' right now.'

Norman backed the roan a couple of yards, turned it and slowly kicked one foot clear of the stirrup. His movements were very deliberate; almost too deliberate, Bart thought. Norman leaned forward, swung one leg over the roan's rump and groped around for the earth. As he did so, he freed his hands and started to turn.

At the same time, Bart, who was suspicious, stepped two paces to one side. He retained his balance and his aim. Norman then brought up a third revolver which had nestled for just such an occasion as this under his left armpit. He trained it and fired it, setting his features in a wolfish expression when he did not achieve his aim straight away.

The revolver shot alerted everyone

who was not alert already. Bart's hat flew off, holed with a bullet. At once the young investigator retaliated, using his Winchester, and Norman jerked and sank to the ground, dying from two fatal wounds in the chest, discharged at a truly lethal distance.

Bart stepped back as the roan went up on its hind legs and then galloped off in a hurry towards the north. No other shots came probing towards the place. Bart went down on one knee beside his victim and assured himself that in fact Norman was beyond aid.

The dark eyes glared at him with all the malice the impostor could muster and then they faded again and rolled in the head before closing for the last time. Seconds were slowly going by. Bart knew that something had to start and start quickly if the ranch hands' plans were not to go awry.

He had heard some slight man-made noise from the other side of the herd before the animals started to bawl and make one another restless. Significantly, the bedrolls around the camp fire still remained unmoved. *If the rustlers did not show themselves in the next minute or so, it would become obvious that there were no men by the fire . . .*

Bart grabbed at Norman's right hand, failed to locate his ring, and reached for the other. He was in the process of tearing it off a finger when the first of the beeves started to rise up off the ground and blunder about.

★ ★ ★

Jake Harris, on the alert and ready to start his offensive, was thinking to himself that there was something wrong with that outburst of shooting and the present set-up. However, as time was so precious in an ambush of this kind he did not have time to reason out what it was that appeared to be wrong.

He stood up in the mouth of the gully a mere few yards from the hollow and the fire and raised his arm. Like an infantry officer, he sent his men forward with another obvious arm movement. They backed him and came up with him on either side.

No less than fifteen shoulder weapons, all fired by experts, put down a veritable curtain of fire around the fading fire. Sparks and small burning embers jumped and sputtered. Hats flew. Saddles bounced and some of them rolled away, displacing the blankets and hats which had been draped over them.

Jake was among the first to see what had happened. He blanched, although there was no one in a position to observe him. He stepped forward another pace and held up his hand. Ten men obeyed him at once, having noticed that there was no return fire or any sort of human movement. Others needed a sharp order to contain them.

'Cease fire, men! The ranch hands must be aware of us. Somebody's given the game away. So back off, go the way you came, an' be cautious because there's no knowin' where the men are who should have been sleepin' down there!'

His voice faded and his men, all reasonably well disciplined, swallowed their disappointment and started back down the gully. The noise of bawling and moving cattle sounded as if the animals were taking over all the action for a time.

The beasts tended to go away from the direction of the gunshots. In doing so, they left the outlaws with a clear line of retreat, but one which was to prove costly. As they got back to the rim of the gully, six rifles manipulated by the drovers who had withdrawn to the south-west briefly belched flame.

Six men absorbed the bullets aimed at them. Two were only scratched, but the other four went down and stayed that way while their fellows continued the slow, watchful retreat down the bottom of the gully.

Jake was quiet now. He had no special instructions to give to his men. They had been outmanoeuvred, and that was not a pleasant thing to happen to anyone in his deadly trade. He knew for a fact that the Circle H had many more than six riflemen in their midst. He was troubled because he did not know where the other cowpunchers were.

Any man's guess was as good as his. They might be hunkered down at the other end of this same gully, patiently waiting to cut down the rustlers from either rim. On the other hand, they might all be somewhere on the other side of the herd, doing their ordinary jobs as nurses to the valuable beasts. As this thought occurred to him, Jake's drooping spirits revived a little. He began to think that they still had a chance of doing a fighting retreat across the stream.

16

BART had the Harries ring back on his finger. Events seemed to be pressing in upon him, but the feel of the circle of gold gave him some comfort. Maybe it would bring him luck, now that it was back on his finger and the thief was dead.

There was no longer any special need for silent movement. To his right, and only a few yards away from him, the nearest and most dour of the beeves were still slowly getting to their feet, bawling at one another and indulging in a little barging and horn wrestling. Already a few dozen of their number were on hoof and pressing hard through the scrub to the north of the selected patch. An occasional shout by an excited cowpuncher confirmed that Blean's boys were on the job and taking it seriously.

Having eliminated Norman and neutralised Winster, Bart was heading for the stream. He knew from what he had seen and heard that the Harries boys had withdrawn in good order; that two or three of the rustlers had been cut down by a token burst of rifle fire as they started to back away from the deserted camp fire.

The gully along which the rustlers were retreating was fairly close on his left. He was aware of this, and that one of the enemy might take time out to scramble up the rim and take pot shots at him. He therefore went to some trouble to stay back from the rim and to keep an eye on the gully itself.

Mounted as he was, he was unlikely to be mistaken for one of the rustlers. His dun was taking him along at a faster pace than they could maintain on foot. If his mount kept up the same rate of progress he would soon be in a position to menace them as they attempted to withdraw across the creek to comparative safety. He hoped that he might make inroads into the numbers of the gang which had so ruthlessly planned to decimate an innocent bunch of cowpunchers. Obviously, Jake and his specially deep feeling of bitterness was behind it all, but the night ambush should never have happened.

As he jogged along between the north side of the gorge and the blundering cattle he wondered where Jake had put himself, and what he thought when confronted by the situation of a few minutes ago. Finding out that he was outgeneralled must have given his confidence a shaking. Perhaps he was thinking more clearly now that he had suffered a setback.

Bart blotted Jake out of his mind. Somewhere along the near bank of the creek the rustlers must have secreted their horses. It was not feasible that they would have crossed the water without them. On the occasion of a reverse they would expect to be near their getaway transport.

Reason suggested that the hidden

mounts could not be far from the creek end of the dry gully. If that was so, then they would not take very long to locate, especially after being disturbed twice by loud bursts of gunfire.

The occasional faint noises in the gully seemed to drop further behind. Bart found himself listening for the Harries cowpunchers instead of the rustlers. The overall calm which temporarily existed between the two warring groups tended to get on his nerves. He had no clear idea where either faction was located, and no time in which to find out.

A scattering of boulders which gave the dun trouble on a short downgrade indicated the creek bank. Bart had to go a little further north to find his way through the dense scrub and tree growth to make his way into the shallows. As soon as they were in a few inches of water the dun began to show an interest in their surroundings. The horse drank cautiously, tossing its head every now and then, and looking first upstream and then down.

By studying the animal and the way it pointed its head, Bart got a useful lead to where the outlaws' horses were located. He had already heard a few sounds which suggested saddle harness when the ear-shattering sounds of gunfire began again. This time, the men under fire were not far from the creek end of the gully. Their closeness brought the young investigator out in perspiration.

He wondered how long he had to try and disperse their mounts before they came bursting into the open and sought to mount up. Fortunately for him, most of the retreating renegades were very keen to return the cowpunchers' fire, and so he was given a few more minutes in which to carry out his task.

The dun tried a couple of tentative steps into the deeper water and then withdrew. There was soft mud at the bottom and the horse was too cautious to trust its weight on that. How else could the waiting mounts be dispersed?

Gunfire was the easiest method, but any sudden outburst might bring a handful of riflemen down on his neck.

Bart fell back on a quieter method. He slipped out of his saddle and plunged his boots into the shallow water. Where he was standing the bottom was fairly firm. By groping about in the water he was able to discover stones. He was breathing hard by the time he had collected half a dozen, but he thought that number ought to suffice.

Straightening up, he stepped further away from the restless horse and began to take aim. His first two stones plopped into water. The third hit animal flesh and after that he was reasonably accurate. It was just after the fifth that a horse did some dangerous prancing and that sent two others off the sandbank and into the water.

The sixth stone was still on the way when the most disturbed horse leapt feet away from the strand and panicked others into going with it. In the darkness it was hard to tell everything that had occurred, but a gambler might have guessed that all the horses had gone into deep water.

Bart then mounted up again and moved his horse some twenty yards further up the near side of the stream where he felt he might have a better chance to pick off swimming men in the immediate future.

★ ★ ★

Three minutes later the first of the retiring rustlers staggered over the end of the dry gully and scrambled down the precipitate slope towards the water. The first two to arrive there quickly saw that their horses had moved on. They had reached that spot about five minutes too late. Now, the horses were too far away for comfort; in deep water and beyond immediate contact.

Bart watched the efforts of the horses as they scattered and swam. A few went downstream. Most swam straight across, heading for the quieter side. Only two headed upstream and they kept well to the middle and egged one another on against a slight current.

The splashing of the first two outlaws as they waded across to the strand attracted Bart's attention. This was the sort of opportunity he was waiting for. He had dismounted by this time and loosely hitched the dun to a willow bole which hung out over the water. With cold deliberation he put the Winchester to his shoulder and took aim. Another flurry of shooting occurred between the gully and the cowpunchers further south, but this time the young marksman was not distracted.

He squeezed, felt the gun kick against his shoulder and shifted his aim at once. It was a good weapon, and one which he was used to. The first outlaw keeled over directly in the path of the second, a bullet having entered his neck and done crucial damage. The second shot struck the next man high in the chest and sent him forward in the water as though he was diving.

The double execution brought a troubled outcry from those who were preparing to follow, and Bart had only a short time in which to move back nearer the bank and crouch low. No fewer than six bullets came homing into his hiding place. All of them went close, but none actually touched him. He sank back against the sloping bank, thankful that he had parted company before this with the dun. This far it had kept out of serious trouble.

Uppermost in Bart's troubled mind was the whereabouts of Jake Harris. Jake had arranged all this and he would surely be in the forefront of the fighting when there was so much at stake. This far, none of the brief glimpses which Bart had had suggested that the outlaw leader had gone down.

If that was so, then Jake must be still on the busy side of the water and, like his men, seeking a way to cross over. What were Bart's chances of picking him off as he tried to make his escape?

Now that such a chance might be coming up, Bart was a little troubled in his conscience. He knew Jake to be a compulsive trouble-maker. A thief, a killer and one set against his kind for life. And yet Bart had known him in prison and out of it, and they had shared confidences. That was what troubled Bart. He had double-crossed Jake, even though the outlaw deserved it. Such a situation did not make for pretty thoughts.

A short period of self-examination made Bart put a brake on his sniping. About thirty yards south of him, most of the gun clashes had already happened. A small handful of escapers had thrown themselves into the water below the sandbank and were swimming across the stream in a variety of unorthodox strokes.

In their effort to get across they made a lot of noise. Bart considered that for a time they had sufficient guns against them to prevent their crossing. As soon as he had reasoned this way, a rearguard outlaw started pumping shells at those who would have prevented the crossing, and he was so accurate that the swimmers made it to half-way. But then a concerted attack upon the rearguard's position shifted him and changed everything.

One after another, the swimmers were picked off by rifles which must have been hot by that time. Bart was mouthing the name of Jake Harris and wondering where he was when he heard a sound upstream of him a few yards. He was not clear what the sound was. Maybe it was just an impression. But someone could have gone past him in the dark with the idea of striking across the water where the opposition was thinner.

As the last two swimming heads went under, Bart concentrated still more upon his earlier impression. His head went this way and that as he checked the bank and the area behind it where the cattle had rested. He might have been jumped himself, so quiet was the moving outlaw, but someone or something made a slight move which panicked the escaper and he fired off his gun in the direction of the sound.

Bart was so surprised he almost gave himself away. After that, he watched the particular spot and kept quiet, even though Ike and Red and others were calling out to him from lower down the bank. A few minutes later he spotted the two horses which had swum upstream. They were re-entering the water on the near side. Something about the way they did so intrigued him. They were behaving as though their reins had been slung over one another's necks . . .

If that was so, then some man had hitched them together and he was planning to use them to get across the water. It could have been anyone, but Bart had this fixation that it had to be Jake. He wondered now how he should act. He perspired as he tried to make up his mind. It was criminal not to let the honest brothers know what was afoot, and, besides, if he did not reveal his presence he might stop a bullet intended for someone else. This decided him.

He unhitched the dun and walked him downstream a short way and then mounted up and rode him on to the sandbank. 'Don't shoot, boys, it's me, Joe!'

'You want we should come across to you, Joe?' Red sounded quite eager. 'Some of the boys have gone back to collect our horses. It's a pity they're on the other side of the camp.'

'Everything's goin' all right, Red. Don't bother about the horses. I want you to give me cover while I'm crossin'. After that, flush the east bank north of the gully. It's my belief there's jest one man waitin' to cross over an' escape, an' he's the one we're mainly interested in. If you see two horses swimmin' over, let them be. So long as I've had time to get ready on the other side.'

By the short silence which ensued, Bart knew that Red was thinking about Jake. 'Sure you don't want us to come over there and give you a hand?'

'No, don't bother, Red. Tidy things up on your side. Make contact with the Blean boys. I don't figure you'll have much trouble after this. The gang is busted for good. There's only the matter of Jake.'

Before the conversation could develop further, Bart sent his dun into the stream and began the crossing. He felt vulnerable, but the line of protecting guns were there, if anyone opened up. As it happened, no one did.

17

THE two horses crossed over some five minutes after Bart had gone clear. Red and one or two of the others alert and on watch felt sure that there was a man almost submerged between the two quadrupeds, but they kept in mind what Bart had suggested and withheld their fire.

One hundred yards back in a thick belt of timber through which any escaper would have to come, Bart Hall had dismounted and was waiting for the final clash with the outlaw leader. Bart's brain was working as though he was running a fever. He wondered how he would be when Jake came up real close and a final crashing of bullets would decide the fate of the two of them.

A slight extra perceptiveness told when the escaper was ashore. Straining ears told that he was coming straight on, hoping to make good his escape in the hours of darkness. Because of encroaching tree branches and the all-embracing darkness, Harris decided to part with one of his mounts.

At a time when Bart was about ready to stir things up, a riderless horse went in one direction and a horse and rider in the other. Although it was done innocent of any subterfuge it baffled the young investigator for a time and took away his confidence.

Behind a stout-boled tree, which he had chosen for his attack point, Bart finally acted in accordance with his conscience.

'Jake! Jake Harris, I know you're there. This is Joe Rider, the man you met in prison! My real name is not Rider, or Arthur, but Hall! I am the real beneficiary named by your uncle who died in Boston! Do I have to say more?'

The sounds of advancing horses still came through the trees, but Jake did not answer straight away. To Bart's surprise the hoarse cry eventually came from the direction which he had discounted. He had thought that Jake was using the other horse, the one which now was likely to be riderless.

Jake did not speak at all. Clearly he had heard the volunteered information and he knew that one or other of them had to die. Surprisingly, Jake's control was the weaker of the two. He started to blast off rifle shots at the imagined source of the voice. This did no harm at all to Bart, who restrained himself from firing and waited for a closer and a better target.

When Jake's gun was empty there was a pause while he reloaded. Then he changed his tactics, asking just one question in a roundabout sort of way.

'When are you goin' to show yourself, jailbird?'

In spite of himself, Bart raised a chuckle. The bit about their meeting in prison was baffling the outlaw. He took a risk and shouted an explanation. 'I was only in prison to find out what Roxy Brownwood wouldn't tell anyone else!'

Jake accepted this explanation and then he was all action. He fired another magazine, reloaded and came on again, aiming at almost every tree and cursing his tormentor for not showing himself. Thirty yards away, he slipped to the ground and sent his mount on ahead of him. Unfortunately, his booted feet landed heavily and that gave away his latest move.

Bart waited until he was less than thirty yards away and then cut him down with a single bullet in the chest. Jake was knocked backwards, but he fought to keep his balance and did so for nearly a minute, before the creeping weakness of death attacked his lower limbs. Bart stayed behind his tree for nearly five minutes, scarcely moving, until the constricted muscles of his upper trunk began to relax.

*　*　*

About ten or fifteen beeves escaped from the vigilant Lazy T team in the night. All the rest were calmed down, rounded up and settled back on their original camping site an hour before dawn. Breakfast was taken early by both teams using the same campfire.

All parties, other than Drag Winster, the survivor, were tired but content. Bart was back. He explained how things had gone on the other side of the creek. He then had Winster brought out from his temporary holding place, the interior of the wagon. He came bareheaded and with his wrists secured, into the midst of the men who had survived the most critical day of their lives.

Bart exchanged glances with the Harries brothers and they nodded for him to do the talking. 'Winster, I have to tell you that all your buddies are dead.'

Drag raised his trussed hands above his head and scratched his bald scalp across the crown. This had been a long night for him and he was still finding it hard to believe that Jake and all his outfit were ready for planting.

Bart resumed. 'Your kind of treachery to an outfit that fed and clothed you can't be tolerated. We could shoot you now, but two things keep you alive. One, I'm takin' you across the creek to bury Jake, and two, you have information we need.

'Now, where do the Circle H cattle go to after they've been rustled?'

Words gushed out of the sole surviving traitor as though their production offered great relief. 'They go to a small new ranch jest over the border into New Mexico territory. Known as the Sombrero, in Caverns County, east of Pecos City. The ranch is run by an honest Mex named Juan Diaz. Him and his wife and three sons have been there since the start.

'They have over two hundred head now, an' when they're not busy they're buildin' new buildings. The *hacienda* is a fine place to see. The Diaz family don't know Jake was a rustler. They took him to be an honest man. They took him to be an honest man. All you have to do is ride over there an' set the record straight. One or two rustlers have been over there, but Jake never let them stay. It's a peaceful place, the Sombrero.'

Winster sounded very disappointed not to have finished his days at the new place.

'I wouldn't be surprised if he still had the same brand on the beeves,' Ike opined morosely.

'That's the truth,' Drag cut in. 'Jake had a thing about not changin' the brand.'

This time no one paid any attention to him. They cut his hands free and allowed him to eat, but there was no one friendly towards him in either trail crew.

★　★　★

Winster buried Jake, the son he had favoured most.

Two of the Circle H boys had suffered flesh wounds, but they had elected to go ahead with the cattle. The

260

drive started several hours late. Bart and his prisoner, Winster, started south again shortly before midday, accompanied by the Blean boys who had helped so much at the critical time.

Later that day, the helpers broke away and went off to their own ranch, leaving Bart and his man to go on alone. Winster, riding five yards ahead, was slumped in his saddle and a picture of dejection. He was troubled because he did not know what sort of a fate old Abe Harries would have in store for him.

Bart was quite certain that Abe was too set in his ways to forgive the veteran hand, but he expected that he would be given a chance to head for the Mexican border before the peace officers got really close.

To Bart, a newcomer to ranching, that *hacienda* over the border with New Mexico territory sounded very desirable. In his present state, of course, he could not expect to be sent over there to manage it. He did not have the experience yet. But perhaps in a year or two, if Ike and Red stayed unmarried, he might have the chance to go to the new place.

It occurred to him as he examined with pride the special ring upon his finger that he did not really mind how Abe apportioned things out. Just so long as he had a hand in the everyday running of the stock and holdings under the Circle H brand.

THE END

Other titles in the
Linford Western Library:

A TOWN CALLED
TROUBLESOME

John Dyson

Matt Matthews had carved his ranch out of the wild Wyoming frontier. But he had his troubles. The big blow of '86 was catastrophic, with dead beeves littering the plains, and the oncoming winter presaged worse. On top of this, a gang of desperadoes had moved into the Snake River valley, killing, raping and rustling. All Matt can do is to take on the killers single-handed. But will he escape the hail of lead?

RODEO RENEGADE

Ty Kirwan

When English couple Rufus and Nancy Medford inherit a ranch in New Mexico, they find the majority of their neighbours are hostile to strangers. Befriended by only one rancher, and plagued by rustlers, the thought of returning to England is tempting, but needing to prove himself, Rufus is coached as a fighter by a circus sharp shooter, the mysterious Ghost of the Cimarron. But will this be enough to overcome the frightening odds against him?

DEAD IS FOR EVER

Amy Sadler

After rescuing Hope Bennett from the clutches of two trailbums, Sam Carver made a serious mistake. He killed one of the outlaws, and reckoned on collecting the bounty on Lew Daggett. But catching Sam off-guard, Daggett made off with the girl, leaving Sam for dead. However, he was only grazed and once he came to, he set out in search of Hope. When he eventually found her, he was forced into a dramatic showdown with his life on the line.